Out of the Grey Zone

Carolyn Joy

ISBN 978-1-0980-6034-3 (paperback)
ISBN 978-1-0980-6035-0 (digital)

Christian Faith Publishing, Inc.
832 Park Avenue
Meadville, PA 16335
www.christianfaithpublishing.com

Unless otherwise noted, all Scripture is quoted from the New International Version. Copyright 1973, 1978, 1984 by International Bible Society, Zondervan TM. Used by permission. All rights reserved.

This is a work of fiction. All characters, organizations, and events portrayed in this novel are either products of the author's imagination or are used fictitiously.

Printed in the United States of America

To my two wonderful friends

Denise
and
Virginia

Introduction

The Grey Zone is that spot between absolute right and absolute wrong. If absolute right is white, then absolute wrong is black. The Grey Zone is that muddy, cloudy area that you know in your heart is wrong but still unwittingly justify why it could be right. The Grey Zone will cause disaster in your life, trauma in your heart, and suffering in your brain. The Grey Zone, at first glance, may appear glamorous and at times may seem romantic; but it promises destruction.

When you have entered the Grey Zone, there is a slow, steady spiritual blinding that takes place that is beyond normal comprehension. When you have lived in the Grey Zone, you realize everyone is one step away from sin. It puts a whole new meaning to the definition of *mercy*. When you pass through the Grey Zone and into the Black Zone you are totally blinded by the very sin that lured you in. It puts a whole new meaning to the definition of *grace*.

The Black Zone becomes the new normal filled with excuses, lies, and hypocrisy. If you are blessed enough to get out of the Black Zone, you will look back with brokenness, shame, hurt, and pain—only to learn that your pride has been shattered, your judgment of sin has been compromised, and your moral strength is only as strong as you choose to make it each and every day. That puts a whole new meaning to the definition of *forgiveness*.

You will also have a keen awareness and knowledge of the control of sin and the awesome understanding in the power of the cross. You will think before you pass judgment on anyone again. Scriptures will have new meaning and come alive with truth. Your relationship with God will never be inconsequential; it will forever be cherished. You will never say "never," for you will have firsthand knowledge that you "never" really know what you will do when you are blinded by sin. *You should always be conscious of sin. You should strive to stay out of the Grey Zone, seeking instead to live in the white zone. Most of all, I pray you learn to discern the difference between the two, as cloudy as it might seem at the time.* Striving to learn the difference puts a whole new meaning to the power of prayer.

This is Amber's story of walking into the shadows and how God eventually delivered her *out of the Grey Zone.*

Last Day Home

Standing in the doorway, I took one last look inside the house I had called home for nearly twenty years. Number 16 Riverbrook Lane was so much more than wood and walls, more than an address on the street. It was a place in my heart. A map of memories filling an emotional scrapbook I would treasure forever. We had raised three kids there, celebrated twenty years of birthdays and Christmases and Thanksgivings. As I perform one last mental walk-through, I can almost taste some of the countless meals that were prepared in that kitchen. Closing my eyes, I see children playing and the sounds of laughter echo in my mind. I feel the warmth that house provided for me on the hundreds of days I came in out of the Boston cold. I can see myself getting children ready for school or church, and as I make one final tour, I realize that every room in that house is a reminder of family...and of life itself.

Of all the cherished memories I will take with me, there are also ones in that 240 months I wish I could leave behind. Experiences and reminders of the past I have purposely left unpacked and in the basement of my mind. Painful recollections of a marriage that was anything but good or happy. When my then husband Bryan and I purchased the home all those years ago, I was a young mother with three babies—a four-year-old daughter, Stephanie, and two-year-old twins, Joshua and Rachel. Married just five years, my relationship with my husband was already at a critical stage. I remember thinking a big new home would somehow bring me the happiness I so desperately longed for. After all that's what fresh starts are for. Every couple has problems, and no husband and wife are without their struggles. Maybe this new beginning in our family would help us iron out some of our marital problems.

I was wrong.

Little did I know at the time, I would face fifteen additional years of heartache, fifteen more years of broken promises, fifteen years of mental and emotional anguish and deprivation.

Looking back, it's all clear to me now. I had married a man just like my father. My mother, like most in her generation, was a stay-at-home mom. Dad was a workaholic and rarely home. Even when he was home, he wasn't really there. Always fixing a car or working on a house project, personal interaction with me or my siblings was rare, unless we were helping him with something. I don't ever remember my father asking me about my day, my feelings, or my friends. What few conversations we had generally focused on him, his work, or stories about his past and upbringing. They were always the same stories. He never had an encouraging or uplifting word. But he would be sure to yell at us when we did something wrong.

My mom took us to church every Sunday while Dad only occasionally attended. His rigid, strict treatment of me produced a rebellious streak at an early age. Embarrassed because of my lack of freedom, and just to prove I was no different from anyone else, I did whatever it took to fit in. Eager to leave home as soon as possible, I worked hard and graduated high school a year early; and yet, in my attempt to free myself from an overbearing and neglectful father, I tried filling that void with a husband. On the surface Bryan was everything I wanted in a man. He was handsome and charming. And best of all he liked me.

But in time what emerged was a man almost identical to the father I had long sought to escape. Like many girls, I subconsciously chose the only kind of relationship that was familiar to me. By running away from my father, I ran headfirst into the arms of a man just like him. By age twenty-four, I had three beautiful children, and like all young mothers, life was hectic and complicated yet precious. I was fortunate enough to stay home with my children, attending all their Little League games, dance recitals, football games, cheerleading classes, and helping them with their homework. On weekends I entertained their friends who came over to play.

Like my own mother, I took my kids to church alone. My husband did not care if they went or not. On the outside we seemed like the perfect Christian family. However, the walls of our home told a much different story. Bryan successfully hid his lack of faith.

Like my father, he never encouraged me or lifted me up.

Like my father, he rarely expressed his love.

Like my father, he yelled about virtually everything, keeping me perpetually running in circles in an attempt to keep peace in the family.

And like my father, he wasn't home much, leaving me to shoulder the burden alone.

Eventually, the accumulated weight of our problems broke our relationship in half, and we divorced after twenty years of marriage. I know that *divorce* is a dirty word in the church. I certainly felt my share of guilt and shame because of our failure. But life, despite our best efforts and purest motivations, does not always turn out the way we plan. The dreaded *D* word wasn't even in my vocabulary when I married Bryan. I had every intention of spending the rest of my life with him. Though I would never portray myself as the perfect wife, I did way more than give it the "old college try." I threw my mind and soul into trying to change our marriage and home into something better. I gave it my all, but it was never enough. A good marriage, any marriage, requires two committed persons to make it work.

Following the divorce, I privately vowed not to date at all in an attempt to be a good example to my children, who were, by this time, high school and college aged. Truthfully, I was so apprehensive of even talking to a man that dating one was the furthest thing from my mind. That, of course, didn't stop men from asking me out. I would repeatedly tell them no, so much so that one man even told me it was as if I had a "Do Not Disturb" sign on my forehead.

But deep down inside me, in the places of my heart no one was allowed to access, there was still a desire to be loved...and married again. Though I had major issues in my marriage, I still loved being married. I think it's probably the security, safety, and stability that marriage and family offer. I was faithful to my husband, never left the kids in order to go partying with girlfriends, and never even gave another man a passing thought. Now, as a single woman, I still longed to fulfill the desire to be complete and "one" with the right man.[1] Even so, I was determined not to suffer through dating every Tom, Dick, and Harry in order to find that man.

I realized that if I was to meet that special person, it was not going to be easy. Most men, and women, at my age were already married. So finding that person would be like finding a needle in a haystack. It was for this reason that I came to believe that if God wanted me to meet someone, he would have to put that person in my life Himself. I naturally reasoned that it would begin with friendship, then a period of dating, after which we would fall in love and be married. Simple as that. I didn't have time for desperate men, bad dates, or meaningless chit-chat. I also didn't want to hurt someone or, worse, get hurt.

Now doesn't that sound like a plan God would want to bless? I certainly thought so.

So though I secretly hated being single, I was willing to wait for God's perfect timing. I was determined not to settle for anything less than His best. My requirements for the next man in my life included someone with godly character and a heavy dose of integrity. If those two standards weren't obvious to me, I would politely decline the invitation. I was waiting for my knight in shining armor, not a loser wrapped in aluminum foil. I already knew all too well what it was like to be married to the wrong kind of person. So next time I was

---

[1] Genesis 2:25

determined to do it "right" or not at all. Being happy and single was better than being married and miserable.

Following my divorce, I chose not to sit and sulk but rather to serve and seek God's best. In the five years after Bryan and I split up, I had become independent and successful. I bought my own home and had a good job and plenty of friends, and I did not need a man to provide for my financial needs. However, I quickly discovered that single moms are in a class all their own and rarely fit in anywhere, even in the church. A single mom's job is caring for her kids, and this makes socializing with others a formidable challenge. We don't blend in well with married adult women, and we certainly don't want to be relegated to the singles group at church. For those reasons and more, I purposely sought out some other single moms, whom I met with regularly. I stayed busy, taking care of my kids, working, serving in the church, and even participating in a number of mission projects and trips. I even hosted a group of single ladies in my home each week for Bible study. At one point, I remember thinking, *If I ever did meet the right man, how was I going to fit him into my busy schedule?*

I also found myself counseling some of the single women concerning the importance of having godly relationships with men. I cautioned them on the damaging effects of premarital sex. We hung out most weekends and on holidays, which can be an especially lonely time for a single mom. It was through this close-knit group that we found the encouragement, support, and sense of belonging we needed.

So how did I end up crying in the doorway of my home of twenty years? Why was I about to leave my church, my friends, and the life I loved?

The best way I can explain it is that my kids were now all in their twenties and living as independent adults. The house was simply too big to justify living there all alone. My son Joshua had graciously agreed to fly from Florida in order to help me with final packing and moving details. Driving home from the airport after picking him up, I walked to the front door and broke down, crying uncontrollably. I was overwhelmed by the thought that this would be my last day in this beloved house.

Now that the packing was finished, here I was again, in the doorway, crying. Though he had a degree in music and biblical counseling, Joshua struggled to find the right words to comfort me. The fact is, I had plenty of reasons to be happy about leaving. I was moving to sunny Florida, America's paradise. No more shoveling snow, outrageous heating bills, or slipping on ice. Ahead were beaches and palm trees. What's not to like?

Eventually, I pulled myself together and finished the final cleanup. I had already sold all my furniture and given most of my extra belongings away. Because it was such a large house, emptying it of its contents and cleaning it from top to bottom was a monumental task. I survived a painful divorce and raised three amazing children into adulthood. Getting a house cleaned and packed would be a piece of cake by comparison. Besides, I was elated about moving south and finding a new home. It would be fun to buy a whole new house full of furniture and furnishings.

After Joshua had strategically packed every square inch of my black convertible sports car, I was finally ready to hit the road. I said good-bye to a few neighbors and then squeezed my five-foot-four body into the front passenger seat. Slipping on my sunglasses I settled in, allowing Joshua to take the driver's seat. Immediately, one of my favorite songs began playing on the radio, "How Great Is Our God." With the radio blasting, we drove south with great expectations of good things to come. My heart was filled with joy, and my jet-black curly hair was blowing in the wind. The past was now in my rearview mirror, and my future was as bright as the Florida sun that awaited me at the end of my 1,500-mile journey.

Life was good. I was happy and content, single and seeking God. What could be better?

New Beginnings and Open Doors

During the long drive from Massachusetts to Florida, I couldn't get my mind off what lay in store for me. I was so excited to move to West Palm Beach, were many of my family members were now residing. There was so much promise there, and it was an ideal place to call home. With forty-seven miles of coastline, not only were the beaches supposed to be the best in the state, but the shopping and dining was said to be exquisite in West Palm Beach. I was also excited to explore the thriving arts community and the many seasonal festivals the city hosted. After arriving, it wasn't long before I saw the rare beauty West Palm Beach had to offer. Every afternoon there were gentle breezes and rains that would blow in from the Atlantic. Living in Boston, I had always loved the water. But I discovered something new in the way the waves seemed to calm the earth as they washed up on the shore, never ceasing. Even today they remind me of God's faithfulness and his mercies, which are new every morning.[2]

---

[2] Lamentations 3:22–23

My first item of business after finding a home and moving in was to secure a good job, which I did almost immediately. I was excited to be hired as an accountant for a large Christian organization called "WeCareWorld International Ministries. This ministry was locally run by Colby Cohen, a well-known and respected member of the West Palm Beach community. Though a CEO, Colby was a down-to-earth boss, a man of character, integrity, and influence. It seemed he knew everybody, and everybody knew him. I had met him and his wife, Ella, at church; and he was more than accommodating in offering me the position at the ministry. In fact, I found Colby and Ella to be two of the nicest, fun-loving people I had ever met.

WeCareWorld Ministries officed out of the church's administration building. I was happy to work for their ministry, which had a close relationship with the local church.

My moving experience had gone so well. And now I found a church and secured a good job. My life had "smooth sailing" written all over it.

On my second day of work, we all attended a seminar sponsored by the ministry. The speaker for the event was a man by the name of Jack Hardie, Colby's best friend. But he was so much more. Jack was retired from the oil business and had also made a small fortune in the Palm Beach Island real estate market. Though having only been in town a short while, I had already heard about this man. His philanthropic reputation preceded him, as he was traveling the world on behalf of WeCareWorld. It was obvious from the moment he walked through the door that Jack Hardie was a confident, driven man. He was handsome for his age, well-built, tall, immaculately dressed in a custom-tailored grey suit, and with a charismatic personality that permeated the room. His full head of silver-and-black hair only added to his distinguished and debonair persona. He looked like a throwback Hollywood leading man from the glory days of cinema. Because I had heard so much about him and his accomplishments, I grew nervous as I noticed him making his way toward my table. I expected him to exude a somewhat aloof, celebrity-like aura. And yet, to my surprise, I found him to be just the opposite of what I had anticipated. Jack was personable, humble, and kind.

"Hi, I'm Jack Hardie," he said with a warm smile and friendly, firm handshake. "You must be the new accountant for WeCareWorld."

Jack gazed into me with bright blue eyes. And though he was friendly, I was still nervous for some reason. I tried to remain calm and confident, though my heart was beating out of my chest. I was hoping it wasn't as obvious as it felt.

"Yes," I replied. "I'm the new accountant, Amber. Amber Gratia. It's nice to meet you, Mr. Hardie."

Jack's firm handshake tightened ever so slightly as he placed his left hand on top as well. "Call me Jack," he said with a wink. My comfort level was somewhat threatened as he continued holding on to my hand. In reality, it only lasted a few seconds. But combined with his penetrating gaze and manly charm, I started feeling awkward.

"Well then, Jack," I said, swallowing hard. "Call me Amber."

I managed a smile, attempting to match his confidence level but failed miserably. At over six feet tall Jack towered over my tiny five-foot-four frame. He finally let go of my hand after one last squeeze.

"You're funny…and cute, Amber Gratia."

Still a bit taken back by his apparent forwardness, I couldn't deny that his personality was warm, inviting, and bigger than life.

He continued, "I'm glad Colby finally found a new accountant. There are so many children that need our help, and there's a lot to be done. Welcome to the team, Amber."

Though Jack's hands had let go, his gaze had not. I caught him glancing my way several times throughout that afternoon. The encounter was a bit unsettling; and yet, since he was a board member, I was glad I had met his approval.

Standing behind the lectern that day, Jack eloquently spoke about his involvement in the mission he was supporting, specifically an orphanage in Thailand. He displayed pictures on a large screen of these precious children, challenging everyone in the room to support them financially. The strong, confident entrepreneur visibly shed tears as he pleaded on behalf of these forgotten children living on the other side of the world.

I thought, *How could such an accomplished, competent man be so humble and unpretentious? How could someone who dined with such powerful and wealthy individuals speak with such compassion and empathy for these impoverished children?* He was a man on a mission, determined to do whatever he could to spread God's love to the ends of the earth.

The room was packed with affluent, influential donors. Each one of them hang on Jack's every word, all of them wanted to help. Jack's deep voice was authoritative, yet soft and compassionate. His many compelling stories even had the "Scrooges" in the room pulling out their checkbooks to donate toward his Thai orphanage.

Jack served as chairman of the board for the ministry. He also served in the same capacity for the Thai orphanage as well as another in Guatemala. He was a pillar in the church I attended, a Bible study teacher, and a speaker at numerous church events. Semiretired, he still owned the aforementioned real estate firm, appropriately named Jack Hardie Properties, with multiple offices up and down the Florida coastline. The business's main office was located in Palm Beach, but he only stopped by when he was bored.

Not long after that seminar fundraiser I volunteered to be a greeter at my church one Sunday. My coworker was a nice lady named Natasha. However, while welcoming a new family and directing them where to go, I looked up to find Natasha had disappeared with Jack now standing in her place. Shrugging it off as a happy coincidence, I continued greeting visitors.

"Hi, welcome to Covenant Christian Community Church (CCCC)."

We took turns opening the door, smiling at everyone who walked in.

"So, Amber," Jack inquired, "are you married?" His bright blue eyes widened with the question.

I hesitated, reluctant to respond. "Um…no," I muttered.

As a divorced single woman, I've always hated that question. But I could usually see it coming from a mile away. Truth is, I hated being single and I also hated being reminded of it every time someone asked me the question. I had been married for so many years that even talking about being single made me feel uncomfortable. But now that Jack had opened the door to the conversation, I knew what question was about to walk through it next.

"Do you have a boyfriend?" he pressed further, raising an eyebrow as he peered over the top of his glasses.

Oh geez! I thought. I didn't owe him an explanation, though my mind frantically searched for one.

"No," I said. My throat and mouth suddenly went dry as I anticipated his next question.

"No?" he acted surprised. "Now how could a pretty girl like you not have a boyfriend? What's wrong with the men in this town? Are they all blind?"

I didn't say a word but instead looked away, attempting to divert the conversation elsewhere and somehow change the topic. But my efforts were unsuccessful. Jack Hardie was not a man to be ignored. Like a seasoned trial attorney, he continued, firing off question after question.

"You mean to tell me that not one man in this town has asked you out on a date? Unbelievable."

It was not the kind of conversation one engages in at church on Sunday morning. How could I explain to him, between welcoming worshipers, that I simply didn't date? How could he possibly understand after what I've been through, any kind of meaningful relationship with a man would be complicated? Maybe the men back in Massachusetts were right. Maybe there really was a "Do Not Disturb" sign prominently displayed on my forehead like a flashing neon light. And if there were a sign on my head, Jack sure didn't see it. Or maybe he simply chose to ignore it. Or maybe it was turned off.

Jack could not possibly have known, or understood, what I was thinking. He was probing, prying me open for information. A man like him doesn't become successful and the CEO of several organizations by being shy or passive.

I scanned the church foyer hoping to locate Natasha and catch her eye in the hopes that she would return and rescue me, but she was long gone. And there I was, cornered in that doorway, no visible exit signs from this conversation.

Turning my attention back towards Jack, I said, "Well, I didn't say no one has ever asked me out. I just said that I am not dating anyone."

That raised another eyebrow. He opened the door for the next churchgoer.

"Good morning. Welcome to Covenant Christian Community Church."

This could be my chance to leave the conversation or at least change the subject. But I had hesitated too long, and Jack dove in again with eager anticipation and determination.

"Oh? So you *had* a boyfriend?"

He obviously wanted to hear the story. But I continued to push back.

"No, I didn't say no one has asked me out, and I didn't say I *had* a boyfriend. I'm just single, happy, and not currently in a relationship."

I could feel my blood pressure rising. I began to sweat. This was not how I envisioned serving the church. Jack was either clueless concerning my obvious uncomfortable body language or he simply chose to ignore it. He continued digging for information.

"Do you mind if I ask how many years you were married?"

Surely my countenance was sending clear signals to him by this time that I was way past being weary of this line of questioning. I took a deep breath, exhaling, "I was married for twenty years."

"Twenty years, huh?" He acted surprised. "And how long have you been divorced?"

My heart rate spiked. I was so over this topic. "Five years now," I said.

At this point, another church member approached the door. It was my turn to extend the welcome, which I did. Jack finally acknowledged that his questions were making me uncomfortable. He smiled, peered over his glasses, and declared, "Well, if I were single, I would definitely ask you out. You are very beautiful, and I cannot believe someone hasn't snatched you up in the last five years."

Unexpectedly, this comment made me blush. For the first time in the conversation, I found myself no longer annoyed. In fact, I found his words entertaining. Curious. Even acceptable. So much so that I thought, *If he were a few years younger and, of course, not married, he would be the perfect catch.* After all Jack was handsome, kind, gentle, and a man with strong faith. Such combined qualities were about as common among men today as a snowstorm in Florida.

Opening the door for another visitor, I sought to close the door to the conversation.

"You see, Jack, I don't need to date the wrong man. I'm quite happy being single."

Liar.

Even though I secretly hated being single, I wasn't about to let him know that. So I reinforced this lie with some solid spirituality. "God will send the right man to me in his time. Most importantly, he must be a strong Christian man. A man after God's own heart and willing to spiritually lead his family. So until that time, and person, comes, I am content to remain as I am."

For the first time in the conversation, Jack was silent. He seemed satisfied with my answer. I observed him that morning, opening the door perhaps one hundred times, greeting each person individually—some with handshakes or hugs, and others with kind words and kisses. He occasionally winked at me, and despite his uncomfortable questions, it made my face blush and my heart beat faster.

But there was something about Jack that resonated within me. While being a well-known man who exuded character and integrity, he also portrayed meekness and humility through his commitment to God's kingdom. When Jack Hardie spoke, the room went quiet and everyone listened. When he made appeals for finances or help at church, everyone responded. Yes, he would be a "catch" indeed. But clearly, he had already been caught, as in forty years caught by his wife, Sarah, to whom he was happily married. At least I now had a model I could use as a standard for the man I would one day marry.

Because Jack was the chairman of the board for my organization, I would have plenty of correspondence with him in the weeks and months to come. His e-mails were always pleasant, funny, and sometimes a bit flirty. I chalked it up to the generational difference in our ages. For certainly this godly man would not be flirting with me. Yet his phone calls soon became more frequent. They started out with business-related matters and soon turned personal, with what he dubbed as "getting to know each other better." My apprehension grew as most of his calls would come when he was in the car. When I finally voiced my concern, he responded by telling me I was imagining it. He said I felt that way because I wasn't used to having a male friend. Jack continually assured me that I could trust him.

I'm not going to lie. I enjoyed our conversations and our friendship. Being an educated man, Jack was always there to offer advice and to help. Being a single woman, it was nice to finally have a strong, wise, male friend to advise me concerning car issues, house problems, appliance problems, financial questions, job-related advice, and, of course, spiritual insight. I had never had a man in my life I could talk to like this. Since he was a happily married man and well respected in the community, we were "safe."

Over the next several months, we became good friends. I knew the relationship was somewhat unconventional, but Jack continually reassured me that it was perfectly normal for me to have godly men for friends. He knew I had been hurt deeply and neglected in my marriage, and he told me he would never do anything to hurt me.

And that was something I desperately needed to hear.

Stepping into the Grey Zone

Though its headquarters was in Tampa Florida, WeCareWorld International Ministries has satellite offices all across the globe, including one in West Palm Beach. The main office had planned a gathering in Tampa for all US-based offices. It would be a two-day training seminar for all presidents, board members, and office workers, including accountants, from each office. We were all strongly urged to come. I acted as point person in our office, contacting my coworkers to see who would be attending.

Not long after my e-mails were sent, my phone rang. Pulling it out of my pocket, I immediately recognized the number. It was Jack. I could feel my stomach begin to churn.

"Oh, hi, Jack."

"Well hello, Amber. How are you today?"

"I'm just fine," I said. "How are you?"

"Just peachy," he shot back in a typical Jack Hardie tone. "So what's this meeting you e-mailed me about, requesting my attendance?"

"Some sort of training with WeCareWorld…I think it's just to make sure we're all on the same page with the main office."

"Who's going to this training?" he asked after a pause.

"Well, from our office, it's just me," I said. "Colby can't go because of a previous commitment that weekend."

Another pause, one so long I thought the call had dropped.

"Well, I don't want you to have to drive three hours by yourself. I'll drive you."

I froze. I didn't know how to respond. It didn't seem appropriate for just the two of us to make the long ride to Tampa together. Not to mention the fact that we would be staying in the same hotel for two long days. This was new territory for me. In my twenty years of marriage, I did not have a single male friend with whom I ever spent time alone. I was uncomfortable with this scenario, especially since Jack was married. My mind was racing, attempting to form a fast response to his offer. But I wasn't good at reacting quickly. So I said the first thing that came to mind.

"Thank you, Jack. That's very kind, but I like road trips alone. I'll be fine, I promise."

This was now the second time I had lied to Jack. Truth was, I hated long car rides alone. Lonely rides made me sleepy. Unfortunately, Jack picked up on the anxiety. He assured me that it was perfectly okay for us to be friends and to travel as coworkers. He guaranteed that his wife, Sarah, would be fine with it and that I was just being silly.

I now found myself in unfamiliar territory. Jack was probably used to driving with coworkers due to his business and his multiple offices all along the East Coast of Florida. Even so, it left me with an uneasy feeling. Of course, I didn't verbalize any of these misgivings or confusion.

Jack broke the awkward silence with a steady voice. "Amber, there is nothing wrong with me driving you there. You're my friend, and I always help my friends."

I could sense that he was beginning to figure me out. Like the first time we met and those piercing blue eyes looked right into me. It seemed that he also had a sixth sense verbally as well.

"I know you mean well, Jack. I just don't think it looks right."

"Your apprehensions are so cute, Amber." Jack laughed. "We are just friends. I know you're not used to having a man as a friend, but it really is okay. Sarah will not mind at all. She likes you. You can trust me. I will never do anything to hurt you."

His words reverberated in my head. *Sarah will not mind. Sarah likes you.* I thought back to my own married life. There were plenty of women that I liked as friends, but I certainly would not have wanted them to go away on a trip with my husband for two days. I had enjoyed getting to know Sarah. She was one of the kindest ladies I had gotten to know. Still, I did not want to travel alone with her husband. I chalked up our difference of opinion to a generational perspective. We simply thought differently about these types of arrangements.

I wanted out of the conversation.

"Oh, Jack. I never said you would hurt me. And I didn't mean to imply that I did not trust you. What I'm trying to say is that other people might get the wrong impression of us traveling together."

"Amber, when are you going to realize that I'm not the kind of man who cares what other people think. I didn't become so successful by worrying about what other people think. What matters is the truth. I happen to know that Sarah would not want you to drive all that way to Tampa by yourself. She will know all about the trip, and believe me, she will be perfectly fine with it." He paused to wait for my response. I could almost feel his bright blue eyes once again peering into my soul. "And just for the record, I don't believe you like taking long car rides alone."

I could hear the smirk in his voice, and he knew I was lying. I didn't want to give in; my gut told me this wasn't right. But no matter what I said, Jack kept pushing. Finally, he suggested that someone else join us on the ride. Nick, another board member, would go to the training and ride with us. I exhaled. Another person in the car offered a degree of accountability. The pressure eased, but that didn't stop Jack from mocking me.

When the time for the meeting arrived, the three of us made the long drive together. Jack was even more fun outside of the office then he was in our work relationship. I was quite comfortable on the long drive since Nick was with us. Nick and his wife, Judy, were among the pillars of the church. Like Jack, Nick was also a retired business-man who served on the board of our church as well as WeCareWorld Ministries. Judy was a women's Bible study leader, and she and Nick were close friends with Jack and Sarah as well as Colby and Ella. It was a tight-knit group of godly leaders in our church, and I felt proud to be friends with them. Colby had earlier expressed his satisfaction that I would be attending the business meeting in his absence. He was even happier that I was somehow able to convince both Jack and Nick to also attend. Since Colby obviously approved of us three traveling together, I reasoned that it must be fine and would appear to be an appropriate travel arrangement.

That first evening of the training seminar, a large group of us decided to go out for dinner. However, Jack approached me after one of the training sessions and said, "Amber, I want to take you out for a nice dinner to thank you for all that you do for our ministries."

His offer caused an immediate wave of heat to rush over me. Processing his request, I concluded that I did not want to go with him alone, yet I still did not know exactly how to express those feel-ings to this hugely confident man. His kind manner was not some-thing I was used to and yet reminded me of what I crave for in a man. I enjoyed the way he looked at me with his bright blue eyes and I didn't know how to say no to him.

"Jack, I'm not sure we should leave the group. After all everyone is going out to dinner together. How would it look if we didn't go?"

I may as well have thrown a feather at a brick wall. He looked at me clearly confused. "I think they will be just fine. Why would any-one care? Besides, they're going out for a late dinner. I prefer eating earlier, and I would like it if you would join me."

My heart ached. Something deep inside me longed to spend time with him. Half of me wanted to go while the other half told me to run. Everyone craved this man's attention and friendship—at church, in business, in the ministry. He was Jack Hardie. Jack Hardie wanted to go to dinner with me, and I was struggling to say no.

"But I already told them I would go out to eat with them," I lied. In case you're counting, that's lie number three.

Jack stared down and looked into my eyes. "Really?" he asked.

I knew I was busted. He clearly did not believe me. The pendulum in my conscience swung back again, and I thought, *Honesty, Amber. Go with the honesty. He will understand.*

"I...don't...I don't really like the way it looks, Jack," I said.

My words betrayed me. I wanted to spend time with him, but at the same time I wanted to maintain the proper role I had as a coworker and friend. I felt a magnetic attraction to him, pulling me away from what my conscience kept telling me.

After a pause, Jack offered a compromise. "I will ask Nick to come with us. After all, we already know it's okay for you to be with two men, right?" Jack smiled and winked at me. He fixed his gaze upon me, looking right into my eyes and said, "Amber, remember something. I am your friend. It is okay to have a man as a friend. You can always trust me. I will never hurt you."

His repeated assurance was beginning to sound like music to my ears. Finally, here was a man I can actually trust. He was a man of power, integrity, character. I had never known a man quite like Jack. I felt for the first time in my life I had met someone who was a role model for me to admire and respect. He was someone I could talk to and who would listen. He seemed genuinely concerned for my well-being, and that was something I've never experienced before. He was able to have deep conversations; and his caring questions, along with his good advice, was a new encounter and something for which I had longed for these many years.

Jack's suggestion seemed like a good compromise. I put myself in Sarah's place and thought about how she would feel if I had gone to dinner with Jack alone. Maybe she was used to it, but I certainly was not.

"Okay then," I conceded. "When should I be ready?"

Jack smiled. "Let's meet in the lobby at 6:00 p.m. I'll tell Nick to meet us there as well."

Now both of us seemed happy with the compromise, as I heard myself blurt, "It's a date!"

I turned to walk away and as I approached the elevator, I sensed I was being watched. I dared myself to glance back, and when I did I caught Jack staring at me with a smile covering his face. I quickly returned the smile and turned away, praying the elevator door would open quickly. It was the longest ten seconds of my life, and I began to sweat. When the door opened, I jumped inside and turned. To my surprise, Jack was standing in the same spot with the same grin draped across his face. I looked down at the floor and pretended not to notice as the doors slammed shut.

*****

Nick was happy to go along for dinner. We met in the lobby as planned, and as I approached the two men, Jack immediately stood to his feet to greet me. I was not accustomed to such kindness and chivalry. Jack was casually dressed in navy-blue dress pants and a pinkish button-down dress shirt. He was a handsome man, and I couldn't help but think how young he looked for his age.

Jack's eyes scanned me from top to bottom as I approached, commenting, "You look very beautiful this evening, Amber." Jack was gifted with words of affirmation, and it made me feel special. "You look fabulous in that dress," he added.

Amber Gratia was definitely entering new territory.

"Thank you," I said. I felt my cheeks get hot and start to blush. "You look handsome too." My voice cracked.

Jack always knew how to break the ice. "Do you approve of the shirt?" His big smile and blue eyes seemed brighter against the pink shirt.

"Yes, it's very nice. Only real men wear pink, you know."

Both men burst into laughter, and I suddenly felt more at ease.

Walking out to the car together, Jack opened the door and gently helped me inside the car. At the restaurant he opted for valet parking but quickly jumped out to open the door for me. As we arrived at our table, Jack pulled out my chair and held it for me until I sat down.

While perusing the menu, Jack asked if it would be okay if he ordered dinner for me. I consented. He knew I liked seafood, so he ordered lobster tail, directing the server to shuck the lobster from the shell so that I wouldn't have to struggle with it. He ordered the best wine and even insisted that I taste his dinner as well, feeding me off his spoon. Although Nick was sitting right there with us, Jack acted like we were the only two people at the table. He embarrassed me by feeding me his banana cream pie from his spoon. This kind of behavior came off as odd to me, but I chalked it up to him being a naïve older man. After all Nick didn't act as if anything was strange. At least I never got the impression that he did. So if Nick was comfortable with Jack's attention toward me, then I figured I should be comfortable with it as well. Besides, he treated me the same in front of other people as he did when we were alone. I was sure that my face was perpetually blushing throughout the whole dinner, but neither of them seemed to notice. This was Jack Hardie, a man who promised I could trust him. What did I have to fear? For me, it was somewhat of an enchanted evening.

We all spent two days in classes and socializing together that weekend in Tampa. During our training sessions, I would catch Jack staring at me, and each time our eyes met, I quickly looked away. And whenever I looked back at him, his gaze remained unchanged. I couldn't help but wonder if others were noticing. I tried my best not to look, but every time our eyes met, I got a strange feeling deep in the pit of my stomach…and in my heart.

4

When Grey Turns Stormy

Jack and Sarah Hardie led a church small group Bible study at their house on Sunday evenings. Around twenty-five people would gather for light refreshments and socializing followed by Bible study. When the next Sunday rolled around, I saw Jack at church and asked him if he needed me to pick up anything for the group Sunday evening. I knew Sarah was going to be out of town visiting friends, so I figured he might need an extra hand to get everything together. He smiled, thanking me for my thoughtfulness, but politely declined my offer, saying he had it all under control. But then around 4:00 p.m. that Sunday, my phone rang.

"Hello?" I answered as my stomach did another one of its all-too-familiar summersaults.

"Hi, Amber, it's Jack. How are you doing today?" His comforting voice put a smile on my face.

"I'm fine." I never knew quite how to respond to him.

"Listen, time has gotten away from me today. I had every intention of going to the store to pick up a few snacks for our Bible study meeting tonight. However, I got stuck on the phone with our Thailand mission friends, trying to drop more supplies to the orphanage, and I never left the house. Would you be able to leave a little earlier so you can stop at the grocery store and pick up some ice cream and toppings?" Then without giving me a chance to respond, he added, "I'll pay you back when you get here."

That was exactly what I was trying to avoid, and my mind raced to provide a solution to this dilemma. First, the trip to Tampa, then the dinner, and now this. Looking back, I can now see the shades of grey creeping in like slow-moving shadows of an afternoon sun. However, at the moment it seemed like such an innocent thing. Besides, at the time, I felt privileged to be Jack's friend and to help him in a time of need, even if it was a small, insignificant request. And it was I who had originally offered to help, so how could I refuse? Even so, I knew Sarah was not going to be at home, and this made me feel conflicted about going to his house alone. I wondered what the other guests would think of my presence there when they arrived. The first few guests would obviously know that Sarah was not at home and that I had stepped in to help him prepare.

Jack didn't seem to think his request was odd at all. I convinced myself I was making a mountain out of a molehill. Maybe I was being too serious about everything. My insecurities from my past left me obsessing about what others thought.

"Sure, just tell me what you need," I said, acquiescing. I jotted down his list and assured him I would take care of it.

"Thank you so much, Amber. You don't know how much I appreciate all your help. You're such a good friend. I can always depend on you."

I loved hearing Jack's voice and was eager to help him out whenever I could. And yet I still could not shake the conflicting feelings within me. I knew he would think I was "being silly" or overreacting if I said I could not come over early to help. I didn't understand why he made me feel so nervous, especially in light of the fact that he continually reminded me that he was my good friend and ministry leader. This confusing struggle still burned in my soul. No one else I knew ever made me feel the way Jack did. While I cherished our friendship, I still felt conflicted. I began sensing there were two Ambers living within me, one rational and one who rationalized.

I contemplated, *What is wrong with me? Why do I always seem to have to make a big deal out of such small things? Why am I being so petty and silly? Of course, I can buy ice cream and bring it to him. It's ice cream for goodness sake!*

Even so, as I got ready to leave, my inner wiring sparked. I knew there was danger in putting myself in this situation. So I called my good friend Kimberly, asking her to come with me. Like Nick at the dinner in Tampa, she would help alleviate my nagging feelings. Kimberly understood my dilemma and immediately agreed to accompany me. We arrived early as planned and helped make the coffee and set up the desserts. Everything went well, and nothing was said about the fact that I had brought a friend along. In fact, Jack seemed thrilled to have the two of us helping him.

*****

Occasionally Jack would unexpectedly show up at the WeCareWorld International office. I thought it was odd how he would show up and blatantly joke with me in front of our pastors, church leadership, and Colby. To me his demeanor seemed flirtatious, but no one else seemed to pick up on it. They were accustomed to his overt, friendly personality. Everyone else seemed to be enjoying Jack, so why shouldn't I? Though I had now been divorced for many years, the lingering effects of my past relationship with Bryan had an unconscious residual effect on me. I couldn't shake the feeling that I needed to loosen up, that I was "wrapped too tight." Admittedly, I was attracted to Jack, as he portrayed so many of the admirable qualities I had desired in a relationship. If only I could find a Christian man like Jack who was available, someone who was funny, kind, and faithful to God. In all the years I had been a believer and church member, I never had a male friend remotely like him. Because of this, privately I began to pray for a man like Jack Hardie.

One day, Jack suddenly appeared in my office, a wide smile across his face. I was in the middle of a busy workday and was taken by surprise at his abrupt arrival.

"Hi, Amber." He grabbed the chair, pushed it closer to the front of my desk, and sat down without taking his eyes off me.

I fumbled over some papers and dropped a stack of paper clips onto the floor. "Hi...hello...Jack. How can I help you?" I stammered.

Jack seemed entertained. He laughed, "I was in the neighborhood and thought I would stop by. That's okay, isn't it?"

I tried my best to appear nonchalant, though I couldn't avoid the strong, alluring aroma of his cologne. His bright blue eyes were locked on me as he leaned on the desk. I wanted to be kind but careful not to appear overly friendly. After all there were people working just a few feet from us.

"Sure, it's okay. You can stop by anytime. I mean, you're the chairman of the board. You can stop by whenever you want." I began playing with a pen on my desk, trying my best to act professional.

Jack launched into conversation telling me about some of the mission projects he was working on. He seemed to really love the children in the Thailand orphanage, traveling there often to help them improve their living conditions.

Somehow, the conversation turned to a ministry that performed surgery on children with clubfeet in third world countries. Then, unexpectedly, Jack leaned over in his chair and reached down toward his feet. I stood up to see what he was doing. He looked up; his expression was quizzical. He then unashamedly took off one shoe and placed it to the side of his chair. Then he took off his other shoe and placed it neatly next to the other shoe. Puzzled, I just stood there speechless, trying to figure out what he was doing.

Then, pulling off both socks, he neatly placed each in a shoe next to the chair. He proceeded to sit up in his chair and lean back, his bare feet now touching the floor. At this point I sat down, not knowing what else to do. Without missing a beat, Jack extended his legs and crossed them, placing his bare feet right on top of my desk.

Needless to say, I was surprised. "Um, *what* are you doing?"

And with that I accidently broke the plastic clip off the top of my pen. Jack laughed.

"See, Amber? My feet aren't so bad. As a matter of fact, you can see they're actually pretty straight. But can you imagine those children with clubfeet and how hard it is for them to walk? I have a hard enough time walking with two good feet."

He sat back, relaxing further into the chair, his shoes and socks still on the floor and his exposed crossed feet comfortably parked on my desk. A satisfying smile spread across his face.

Still unsure, I put down the broken pen and picked up another.

"Jack, I know you certainly did not drive all the way here to show me your feet. Now put your socks and shoes back on."

I accidentally popped the plastic clip off of another pen, quickly tossing it aside in hopes that Jack wouldn't notice. Although I was laughing, having a man's bare feet on my desk was still a first for me and admittedly made me feel uneasy. I feared someone would walk by my office and get the wrong idea about Jack's humorous attempt to make a point about missions. But as usual he appeared unfazed and oblivious to anyone else's presence. In fact, he seemed quite entertained by my discomfort and made it known by laughing at my embarrassment. But though uncomfortable, it occurred to me that I was thoroughly enjoying this newfound attention and friendship and I couldn't deny he was fun to have around.

Jack glanced at the second broken pen. "Having pen problems today, Amber?" he asked.

I would discover in time that there was little Jack Hardie ever missed. He bent over and began putting his socks and shoes back on.

"Oh, they're just cheap pens…they break easily," I countered, reaching for yet another one.

Jack finished putting on his socks and shoes and stood up. Being a classic type A personality, he neatly pushed the chair back against the wall in front of my desk, lining everything up just the way he had found them. Though he was twenty years older than me, he radiated a much younger persona.

"Thank you for cleaning up, Mr. Hardie," I remarked, breaking the silence. I caught myself smiling as he walked toward the door.

Jack giggled. "You are very welcome, Ms. Gratia. However, the room is not yet clean." Casting his eyes toward the floor, he chided, "You will have to pick up these paperclips." And with a wink he disappeared out the door.

I sat there stunned at his unexpected visit, laughing at myself as I gathered the paperclips up from the floor. I could hear him briefly joking with each person as he made his way out of the office. Everyone in the WeCareWorld and the CCCC offices always enjoyed a visit from Jack Hardie.

And I was no exception.

5

Late for Lunch

One of my many responsibilities at the ministry was to occasionally join Colby in meeting with potential donors. On one of these lunch appointments, Jack had also been invited. But on the day of the meeting, Jack showed up at the office instead of meeting us at the restaurant. As he was about to leave, Colby was gathering his papers for lunch when he ran into Jack in the hallway.

"What are you doing here, Jack? Why aren't you at the restaurant?"

"I'm not going. I don't have the time today. You can meet with them and tell them about the needs of the ministry," Jack said.

A little disappointed, Colby nevertheless accepted Jack's explanation. After all Jack could do whatever he wanted, whenever he wanted. He was a busy man with multiple ministries and business responsibilities. He was pulled at from all sides, which is why getting any time with him at all was considered a bonus. Colby knew this and understood how hard it was to pin Jack down.

"Oh, I'm sorry you can't come, Jack. We'll miss you." Colby snatched up his briefcase and headed out the door, but not before turning to see me moving things around on my desk. "Meet you at the restaurant, Amber," he said. Then he shook Jack's hand. "Bye, Jack. I will let you know the outcome of the meeting."

But Colby wasn't the only one who was surprised at Jack's arrival there in the office.

"Is there something you need from me, Jack? Because I need to leave for the restaurant in a few minutes." I knew I needed to hurry and make it to the lunch, but something inside me also wanted to stay and see what Jack needed.

Jack just stood there. I could tell he had something on his mind. He looked down at me with a serious face.

"I wanted to show you pictures of my last trip to Thailand," he said.

Though his timing wasn't exactly perfect, I found it hard to say no. Everything he did was so interesting and remarkable, and the opportunity to see what God was doing in the orphanage in Thailand was hard to pass up. My heart was also once again warmed by his attention. "Okay, I have just a few minutes." I motioned for Jack to sit in one of the two chairs in front of my desk. But instead, he began moving the chairs around in the office, placing his chair right beside mine.

Jack's close proximity made me feel uneasy, but it didn't seem to bother him. He proceeded to hand me picture after picture, our fingertips regularly brushing against one another. In fact, he was close enough that the hairs on his arm rubbed against my skin as he told me the story of each photo. I began to squirm with this awkward closeness, but he just kept talking. I felt flustered by our close proximity, but whenever I attempted to move away, he just inched closer, continuing to brush my arm with his. I consciously tried to reason away any unnerving thoughts about this.

Jack definitely had different boundaries than the boundaries I was used to. As we looked together at each picture, he spoke gently to me about each one. He seemed genuinely interested in my response to each photo. And I was interested in each of his stories. This kind of dialogue was new to me, and I secretly loved it. I loved it so much that I didn't quite know how to tell him I had to get going or I would miss my lunch with Colby. He just kept talking. I was torn between my work commitment and the attention I so desperately wanted to give this man…and the attention I so desperately enjoyed receiving from him.

I knew Colby was expecting me. I also felt guilty that Jack and I were now completely alone in the office. Now I would be late for lunch as well. I knew I had to say something, so I mustered up my courage.

"Jack, I love these pictures and I thoroughly enjoy hearing you talk about each one, but I am expected at the lunch. I am going to have to leave now." My sudden announcement broke his train of thought.

"Oh…yes, of course. You had better go if Colby is expecting you."

When I finally broke free and said good-bye, my heart was racing. I felt overwhelmed by his presence. Hurrying out of the office and driving across town, I arrived at the lunch so late that the three of them had already finished eating.

Colby looked up at me, "You're late, Amber. I began to think you weren't going to come."

I just managed to fake a smile. Shrugging my shoulders, I nervously explained, "Well, you know how hard it is to get away from Jack when he has something on his mind,"

As I sat down in the lone empty chair at the table, Colby laughed, "Yeah, I know exactly what you mean."

Once again, I was the only one who felt awkward at Jack's actions. Colby didn't think his office visit was odd, and that made me think I was overreacting…again. As one of his closest friends, Colby knew Jack better than anyone. However, I was beginning to think I knew Jack better. Or perhaps neither of us *really* knew him at all. My thoughts were interrupted as Colby continued, "Now let's order you some lunch, Amber. You must be hungry."

6

Jealousy

It was about this time that Jack began giving me books to read. Many of the children in the orphanage in Thailand would have been sold into human trafficking had we not protected and provided shelter for them. We're talking about families so poor that many of them sell their older children for a few dollars in order to support the younger ones. Other times they are tricked into believing the child will be given "work," and their wages will be sent home to help them support their family. But of course, it was all a lie, an elaborate ruse to obtain more victims for their evil endeavors.

Jack provided several books to read to help educate me concerning this horrific topic. Most of them contained extremely graphic and gruesome information. But because I was employed by an international ministry that helped such children, I reasoned that he simply wanted me to be informed about what was going on in these foreign countries. Even so, it was unsettling for me to read such sexually graphic material. It was also awkward when I would return a book to Jack and he would then talk to me about the stories. I chalked it up to his gallant personality intersecting with my prudent disposition.

As time passed, I took on more and more responsibility for Jack's mission project adventures. In addition to working together, I also began voluntarily helping him launch his other ministry ideas. Jack always had a global strategy in mind, and I was able to orchestrate it all from our hometown office. I administered all the paperwork, and he did all the traveling, heading out to Thailand at least every other month to check on the kids and the projects.

Ultimately, Jack began telling me that his wife Sarah was jealous of our relationship. He even asked if I would be willing to come to his house in order to spend some "girl time" with Sarah. He suggested I could teach her how to use a computer so Sarah could help me with some of the paperwork and mailings for the mission projects. This seemed like a good idea, as it would put her mind at ease concerning my relationship with her husband. So naturally, I agreed, going to their home and teaching her about Excel spreadsheets. Sarah was always kind and sweet to me, and she was eager to learn as well. However, she had little interest in administrative work, and it showed as she would never follow through with tasks. I would have to go behind her to catch up with the spreadsheets and mailings she had agreed to take care of but rarely did.

I really never understood why Sarah would be jealous of me as she was a strikingly beautiful, godly, and sweet-natured woman. I used to think she and Jack looked like Barbie and Ken. Both were well-respected, lived in a beautiful home, helped people around the world, and at least gave the impression that they had the ultimate marriage.

But since Sarah had become jealous of my working relationship with Jack, he asked me not to send correspondence to his personal e-mail anymore. Instead, he told me about a separate e-mail account he used exclusively for his mission projects. He preferred that I e-mail him on that account since Sarah did not check his business e-mail account. That way Sarah would not be jealous of our working arrangement and correspondence. And because it seemed like an easy solution to a potentially volatile issue, I agreed.

I also told myself that I certainly didn't want to cause Jack any distress in his marriage. Besides, I wanted to believe Sarah was being silly since there was nothing to be jealous about. Although I was fond of Jack's professional companionship, I had no plans to ever seek after an older, married man.

I was enjoying all the benefits of our friendship. But somewhere in the back of my mind, I knew I was passing boundaries into the Grey Zone. I justified our deepening friendship by reminding myself of all the good we were doing around the world. We even began joking about the Grey Zone. When his friendly innuendos got a bit inappropriate, I would remind him to stay out of the Grey Zone. He even began confessing when he knew he was entering into the Grey Zone. But after a while, this Grey Zone became normal for us.

It even began to feel glamorous.

Romancing the Grey Zone

Over the next several weeks, Jack would call me on my cell phone for various reasons, usually ministry related. And every time he called my heart skipped a beat. My mind wrestled with the growing feelings within, and my first instinct was to not answer and simply let it go to voicemail. But my feelings bypassed rational thought, and I always ended up taking his calls. And that Monday's call was no different.

"Hello?"

"Hi, Amber." His deep, husky voice triggered fresh emotions in my heart, and I struggled to respond.

"Oh, hi, Jack. How are you?"

I tried my best to sound professional, not wanting to appear affected by his call.

"Much better now that I am talking to you," Jack said in his typical unassuming manner.

It took a moment for that to register. I thought, *Wow, did Jack just say that to me? No, wait. Maybe he meant that professionally. Because he has some task he needs me to help him with. Perhaps he needs an administrative favor or a new project he wants me to work on. Or perhaps something is troubling him and he needs me as a work colleague.*

Truth is, I never quite knew how to interpret his seemingly flirtatious conversations as they appeared ordinary to him. After what seemed a long pause, I broke the silence. "What do you mean? Is something wrong?"

Jack continued in his matter of fact style. "No. I just love hearing your voice. When I hear it, I picture your big smile."

Jack was a man of words. He knew exactly what to say to lift my spirits, make me feel special, and make me smile inside and out. He had the unique ability to make me feel like I could conquer the world. He had made a habit of encouraging me, convincing me I was much more wonderful than I believed myself to be. I treasured our long conversations and the knowledge I gleaned from talking with him. However, it did not escape me that he was a flirt. That was what confused me. How could this godly man, a man whom everyone idolizes, also be a flirt? It didn't make sense. I reasoned that I must be magnifying his words through my own emotional grid and letting my feelings get away from me. Surely he meant no harm. He was just being playful and nice.

"Jack, don't get grey on me." I laughed.

This prompted an outburst of laughter from him, and he quickly changed the subject, something he was very good at doing. "I was calling to ask if all our Thailand children presently have sponsors. I received a phone call from a friend last night who wanted to sponsor a child in the orphanage."

I was glad to move from the Grey Zone and back into ministry talk. "Yes. They are all presently sponsored. However, there are a few donors who have had some financial problems. So I don't know how long they'll be able to continue to keep their commitment." I was proud of my professional response.

Jack's voice then turned even more businesslike. "Well, I will give you their contact information, and you can reach out to see what they would like to do with their donation."

"Perfect," I answered. "It's always a good idea to have back-up donors in case we lose one."

"Thank you for all your help, Amber. I hope you realize that I couldn't do this alone. You are such an amazing asset to me, and I appreciate all your help. We make a good team."

His words were an affirmation to me that I was in the right place in my life. I loved helping Jack, and I loved assisting charitable organizations. In fact, it was something I was very familiar with. I had been involved in some aspect of ministry work almost all my adult life. When my kids were little, it was children ministries. When they hit the teenage years, it was youth ministry. And when they got older, I transitioned to other ministry opportunities at church. However, this kind of ministry was new to me. Organizing local donors for worldwide opportunities was a unique, challenging, and rewarding responsibility.

"Thank you, Jack, I love doing this."

I expected the call to end right there, but Jack continued, "Now, I know I am going in the Grey Zone with this, but I almost can't help it, Amby."

Jack's repertoire of affectionate nicknames for me was growing.

"You are an amazing person. You balance your job and then voluntarily help me with multiple tasks that I would never be able to do alone. I know you work till the wee hours of the morning getting it all done. You are always kind and you always lift my spirits, even if I am having a rough day." Jack paused, as if waiting for my response.

But I didn't know what to say as I processed his kind, affirming words, which I had grown to sincerely believe.

"I just cannot thank you enough for all the time you devote to me and how you help the poor and needy around the world. I know I can always depend on you. When I am feeling down and over-whelmed with the burden of responsibility, I know I can call you and your voice makes everything better. You are such a kind and gentle person. So don't be upset with me for going grey, as you would call it." He laughed. "But just know that you are more than a coworker, you are my good friend and I love you."

Jack's words penetrated my heart. Oh, how I needed to hear someone say that. It felt so good to be appreciated. In that moment, I wasn't thinking Grey Zone but rather words that described a true friendship. My heart was beating with warm, uncertain feelings that I struggled to understand. Navigating between my heart and mind revealed a divide that seemed to be growing. I immediately told myself that the "love" he described meant love between friends, not love between a man and woman. Certainly not the kind of love you experience when your heart is beating with intimacy.

It was important that I responded to him with a clear mind and not with the heart of a woman whose emptiness was being fulfilled.

"I am not upset with you at all, Jack. I am so honored to be your friend, and I am privileged to work beside you as you travel the world to help the people who depend on you. Thank you for trusting me with such an awesome responsibility."

"So you are not mad at me for entering the Grey Zone?" he joked.

"No, silly," I said. Hesitating before speaking again, but in that moment, my head gave way to my heart. "You're fine. It's not grey."

We hung up, and I reasoned once again that Jack's overly friendly accolades were a result of his genuine friendship. I was really beginning to understand him and believed him when he said he really enjoyed working with me.

What I did not know at the time was that there is a real sense of intimacy that takes place between a man and a woman through "talking." In fact, that is where it all began. Unconsciously, my heart secretly started beating in sync with his through these conversations. His words gained access to a place inside me, awakening feelings that had lain dormant for decades. But I was either too naïve or too blind to see it. The Grey Zone Jack and I were flirting with began to take on darker shades. And the darker it grew, the more enchanting it became. I told myself that I should, and could, keep it above reproach at all times. After all we were both grounded in our faith.

But I privately wondered if one day the solid ground beneath our feet would open up and swallow us both.

8

E-mails

Jack traveled to Thailand every other month to check on the children in the orphanage. He typically brought them medical supplies and made sure they were getting enough food. He also oversaw multiple orphanage repairs and would check in on the workers and the status of the building and grounds. Each trip was packed with activity and meetings and he always took a lot of pictures too.

While he was away, Jack never called but he often e-mailed to keep me posted on the status of operations over there. I checked my e-mails daily to download the pictures he would send. I always loved seeing pictures of those precious orphans. Some days we would be in constant communication, while at other times I wouldn't hear from him for a week or more. I loved hearing from him and also seeing how the children were blossoming with the love and care the sponsorship program provided for them.

One such e-mail I received included an update on the children's' status and the building progress. I quickly returned the e-mailed hoping to catch him at the computer.

"Hi, Jack. Hope all is well with you and the children. Please send my love to them and ask them to write to me."

Only a few seconds, and I was surprised to receive a direct reply.

"Hi, Amber. All is well. The children are doing great. The building progress is coming along just fine. I have taken lots of pictures today with the children. I know you will love seeing them."

I was so happy to hear from him. I quickly typed another response.

"So glad to hear all is well. Don't forget to give the children the letters from their sponsors and ask them to write before you leave so you can carry the letters home."

Jack immediately responded, *"I know, Amber. I know the routine by now.* ☺ *"*

A smiley face. He sent me a smiley face. I didn't even know he knew how to make a smiley face. It made me chuckle, warming my heart. Then suddenly, another e-mail popped up.

"By the way, Amber, I have to admit something. I really miss you. I know it is really strange, and I should not be saying this, but I cannot get you off of my mind. I get this strange feeling when I think about you. I know you will say I am going grey, but I just can't help it. Forgive me for feeling this way, but I love working with you, and I wish you were here with me to help me with the orphanage. I can't wait to take you with me on one of these trips, so you too can visit the children."

His words knocked me back in my chair, and I had to catch my breath. *Did I read that right?* I leaned forward and read it again. A strange feeling began growing in the pit of my stomach. Perhaps I was misreading it, or subconsciously placing my own emphasis on individual words. I held my breath. Then let it out slowly and read again. *Nope, pretty sure I am reading it right. And yes, that was definitely grey.* I didn't answer him back as I didn't know what to say. *Maybe if I just ignore it, he would not know whether I had received the message.*

I quickly shut my laptop and walked away, as if that, somehow, would make it go away. How was I supposed to respond to that… to *him*? On into the evening, my mind was spinning, imagining all kinds of thoughts. I convinced myself he was probably just feeling lonely and tired from the long trip. Travel like that does take its toll on a person. So, in that context, it was probably no big deal. I once again justified his flirtatious personality by citing our generational differences. His generation was free with words and not intimidated by what other people think, while my generation was more literal due to e-mail and texting. I dismissed my suspicious feelings. No harm, no foul. Jack was a man of faith. And I could trust him.

A Healthy Relationship?

Jack had developed a number of endearing names for me, and would refer to me as "Amber Girl" and "Precious Amber." He even shortened my name to "Am" at times. He told me over and over that I could trust him. He repeatedly assured me that he would never hurt me. It was everything I needed and wanted to hear. Words I had longed to hear all my life.

All during this time, Jack served multiple roles in my life—as my Bible group leader, spiritual advisor, and missions ministry partner. We were a part of the same church, attended all the same parties, and had all the same friends. He would periodically come to my house for ministry type meetings, and I regularly went to his house for Bible study and other social gatherings. We hosted dinner events together to raise funds for the orphanages in Thailand and Guatemala. Jack became interwoven into the fabric of my life.

Life was good, and I was enjoying it. I had a great job, I was part of an impactful ministry, and I had a good reputation in the church and community. All of these achievements brought a deep level of satisfaction. I was so glad I had moved to West Palm Beach, Florida.

In addition to all this, my grown children were all wonderful, successful, intelligent people. Looking back, I had no regrets as a mom. I gave everything I had to my kids, sacrificing for them and raising them in an environment of unconditional love. I also was grateful for having brought them up in the nurture and admonition of the Lord. In time each of them embraced a personal faith in Christ. As adults they had all married amazing spouses. It gave me great joy to see them prosper in their marriages and families. My son, Joshua, and his wife, Shanna, both had music degrees and were serving in our church as choir directors and music ministers. Since my other kids were living elsewhere, it was an added bonus to have Joshua and Shanna near me and, now, a part of the same church. My family's success, my job, and my new state of affairs made me realize that I could not have been in a happier place than I was at this time.

My job at WeCareWorld was a rewarding one, as I loved helping orphaned children around the globe. I saw my role as a much-needed one, facilitating ministries that helped change the lives of thousands of needy kids. It didn't matter how large the project, I loved taking on each administrative challenge and enjoyed the sense of responsibility it bestowed on me. And I was enjoying working with Jack and the way these projects connected our relationship. Jack's dynamic personality endeared him to everyone. People loved to be near him and *with* him. The Bible study class he taught could hardly be contained, as it was bursting at the seams with people who desired his friendship, leadership, and attention. And in a twisted sort of way, I felt "privileged" to have the kind of friendship with him that others were seeking.

Jack and I were friends and coworkers for over two years, and our relationship only strengthened as time went on. On occasion, I entertained thoughts of ending my working relationship with Jack, but honestly, I was enjoying everything about it. I admitted to myself that although I had "feelings" for Jack, I had everything under control. After all, we were two good, sincere people. Everything would be all right.

Ours was what I considered a healthy relationship. We never did anything "wrong." We were just really close friends. We certainly had never crossed any sexual or physical boundaries. We both were strong Christian believers, serving God, our church, and our worldwide ministries. This is what I genuinely believed. However, I had forgotten that most of Satan's temptations are designed to catch people off guard, even people who think they are well-grounded and rooted in their faith. He targets people who know right from wrong and who try to making godly choices. But none of us are immune to his schemes. None of us are exempt from deception, not even a sincere woman like me.

One of the first clues to this deception came about two years into my working relationship with Jack. I opened my computer one morning to discover an e-mail from Jack's wife, Sarah. The e-mail was kind but to the point.

"Do not be overly friendly to my husband. Keep your e-mails brief. Only speak about business and do not get personal. Oh, and do not tell Jack I e-mailed you!"

"Whoa!" I whispered. "Where did that come from?"

To say I was shocked would be an understatement. I would agree that Jack and I could be overly friendly and that deep down I acknowledged a level of occasional inappropriateness, but I had absolutely no intentions of stealing anyone's husband. If there was ever a line in the sand not to be crossed, it was to not fall for a married man. Jack and I had established a seemingly healthy relationship over the previous two years, and I thoroughly enjoyed his friendship. But I had never even been on a date with a man, any man, since my divorce seven years earlier.

So to think Sarah was somehow implying that I wanted her husband came as a complete shock to me. And in spite of her request to keep silent about this correspondence, I did the exact opposite. I wanted to get to the bottom of this shocking e-mail. So I called Jack and told him about it.

I didn't know when I told Jack about Sarah's concerned communication with me that I would be opening up a huge can of worms. To my complete surprise, Jack proceeded to verbally vomit some very unpleasant, and private, information. He proceeded to confess that he and Sarah did not have a good marriage. Their public image of the happy, Christian marriage was all a facade. He said Sarah was jealous of every woman in his life, not just me. He then began naming all the other women that I knew who made Sarah jealous. Jack reminded me about seemingly innocent situations that Sarah twisted into flirtatious or romantic scenarios. Then Jack dropped a bombshell by telling me he had wrestled with Sarah's jealous and accusatory nature since the beginning of their long marriage.

"To be honest, Amber," he admitted, "I never really loved her."

This news blindsided me like an unexpected ocean wave, the sheer force of it shocking me down to my core. He went on to explain that everyone believed Sarah to be such a sweet, caring person but that at home she was a perpetual nag, never happy, and always complaining. He claimed she criticized him for everything he did, always trying to change him into someone he wasn't.

Though I acknowledged the reality of Jack's words, my ears could hardly take in such unbelievable assertions. But why would someone like Jack Hardie ever want to make up such a narrative? Because of his stellar reputation and my personal experience with him, I had every reason to accept Jack's version of the story as accurate and true. The more he talked, the more it all began making sense. I had spent lots of time with the two of them, and looking back, they never did seem to be affectionate toward one another. They never traveled together or, outside of the Bible study, ever worked in ministry together. Although they were always cordial and kind to one another, there were never any public displays of affection typical of other couples. I had written it off as being the way their generation acted. But upon reflection, I realized I never saw them holding hands, embracing, or even standing with their arms casually around each other.

But while it all seemed to make sense, Jack's revelation was nevertheless a difficult pill to swallow, especially since, by all appearances, Sarah was a faithful, beautiful, sweet-natured woman who always seemed to have it all together. She was quite athletic for her age, always dressed fashionably, and looked much younger than she actually was. In their Bible study class, she was the first to pray, always offering insightful answers, and was always willing to serve. She had always been kind to me, treating me with love and grace. But now I had another story concerning their marriage, a behind-the-curtain backstory revealing the true nature of their relationship.

Understandably, Jack was furious with Sarah for sending that e-mail to me.

10

When Grey Turns Black

One of my ministry responsibilities was to collect letters, notes, and pictures from the sponsors (here in the US) for the children in Thailand. When Jack would travel overseas, he would take that correspondence with him to the children. Then the kids would write notes, take pictures, and send them back to the sponsors. Jack was again getting ready for another long international trip. This time he was traveling first to Guatemala to check on the orphanage there. His primary contact there was Juanita, a Guatemalan missionary woman who ran the orphanage. Jack would spend a week in the mountains ministering with Juanita and then head off to check on the Thailand orphanage for another two weeks.

I had spent hours producing a DVD about the Thailand orphanage using previous video footage of the children, the orphanage grounds, and of Jack providing information on sponsoring the children. It was an effective media tool, complete with heart-touching pictures, videos, and music. While I was at home putting the finishing touches on the DVD, my phone rang. Looking down at the phone, I got that strange feeling in the pit of my stomach again. It was Jack.

"Hi, Amber. How are you doing today?" Jack sounded much more serious than normal.

"I'm fine, thank you, Jack. How are you today?"

"I'm fine, but I have a big favor to ask of you." He hesitated, as if searching for words. "Amber, could you please bring the papers and the DVD to my house on Tuesday morning?" He asked with such kindness and appreciation that it always made it hard for me to say no. And yet I already knew I did not want to go to his house. Jack had informed me he would be taking Sarah to the airport early that morning so she could visit her family while he was away overseas. I definitely did not want to find myself at his house alone with him. There was a brief dead silence on the phone as I thought fast for an alternate solution.

"Um, how about meeting meat the office on Monday?" I suggested. I felt the office offered a safer setting and was clearly better than going to his house.

"Well, I do not know if I will have the time to go all the way to the office on Monday," Jack said.

"Well then, how about—"

But before I could finish my sentence, he calmly interrupted me. "You know, Amby, I am quite busy these last few days. I will be away for the next *three weeks*, and putting all these last-minute details together for multiple ministries in third world countries isn't the easiest job in the world. You are always so accommodating. But as you know, trying to organize the food drops, medical supplies, and the supplies for the orphanage is just overwhelming. Not to mention, when trying to talk to anyone in Thailand or Guatemala, it's like dealing with the Flintstones over the phone."

Jack hesitated while I struggled to find an alternate solution in my mind. Then he continued, "If it's too much trouble, I will understand. I just thought you might help me out since there is so little time before I leave."

For a retired businessman, Jack was unusually busy. And if you wanted something done, Jack was the person to do it. He could balance family, church, Bible studies, being chairman of the board positions, and managing multiple mission trips with ease. I felt an enormous sense of guilt in saying no to his request, especially since the one asking was Jack Hardie. No one said no to Jack. People follow leaders with vision, and Jack was a living example of that. This made me want to accommodate any and all of his ministry needs.

Knowing that Sarah was leaving on Tuesday morning and would not be home made me uncomfortable. So I proposed a compromising solution. "I would love to help you out, Jack." I spoke slowly and precisely. "What if I just bring the materials to your home over the weekend and we can work on it then?" I was proud of my answer and thought the compromise made perfect sense.

But Jack didn't. "No, that won't work at all. We have previous plans. Sarah and I will both be busy all weekend before we both leave." I could now sense the frustration in his voice. He then became more assertive. "I will have painters here Tuesday morning, painting the front entrance, so you could come and help me straighten out all the last-minute items I have regarding Thailand. I would really appreciate this, Amber."

I felt trapped. What else could I say? Jack was asking, even pleading, for my help. What was I going to do? Leave him hanging? Let the ministry suffer? How could I say no? Anyone else at church would have jumped at the opportunity to help Jack, and I wanted to help him too, but there was something about the way he treated me that put a knot deep in the pit of my stomach. I wasn't used to feeling this way. His accolades and compliments gave me a confidence that was glaringly absent in my past life. I had never known a friend like Jack. Here was a man who seemed deeply interested in my well-being. Our relationship seemed safe.

And so I reluctantly agreed. After all, there would be other people at the house—painters. Several of them. That helped to lower my concerns and raise my comfort level a bit. I no longer feared Tuesday morning's meeting.

However, that small single decision would change the entire course of my life.

Painted into a Corner

Arriving at Jack's home, I had been asked to park in the rear of the house and enter through the back door. It didn't seem like an odd request, as the painters were busy working on the front door. The driveway horseshoes around the back of the house where the patio is located, providing entrances leading to the spare bedroom, kitchen, living room, and master bedroom. I figured I would enter through the back kitchen or living room door. As I pulled up to the back driveway, the black gate opened on cue. I parked near the basketball court, got out, and walked around the court, past the pool and the hot tub.

I was beginning to have second thoughts about my arrival. It was the end of August and a hot summer day. I was already sweating as I walked through the yard. Through the lush landscaping, I could see Jack standing there, that familiar smile spread across his face. He looked so handsome in his pressed blue jeans (with the crease down the middle that he himself ironed each day) and black fitted T-shirt. His brown leather belt with gold buckle and brown leather sport shoes only added to his youthful appearance. His suave exterior and physically fit body made him look much younger than his age. Though twenty years older than I, you would never know it. As I drew closer, I could smell his cologne.

Jack was waiting for me on the lanai, situated just off the exterior master bedroom door. I felt a bit apprehensive entering through the bedroom, but quickly dismissed the thought of anything inappropriate. We greeted each other on the lanai with a hello and a quick hug. Then he escorted me right through the bedroom and into the living room. There were, indeed, painters at the house, but they were outside, painting the outside entrance. I was under the impression they were going to be inside. But I was relieved to know they were there and that I was in the living room.

Jack wanted to watch the DVD I had completed, so I played it for him on a nearby laptop. As we watched the video together, Jack was standing close to me, and at times his body slightly touched my arms and shoulders. My heart began to race in the context of this seemingly compromising situation. But again, I managed to quickly dismiss the inappropriate gestures.

How could I say no to any of his requests or imagine anything unethical about our circumstances? I began feeling guilty for having such critical thoughts.

After viewing the video, Jack thanked me for doing such a good job, remarking that he could not do this important work without me. Of course, I was thrilled to receive his gratitude and accolades. I gave him the rest of the materials he had requested and began making my way back through the master bedroom and out the back door. However, right before reaching the French doors leading to the lanai, Jack suddenly stopped me to say he had some pictures he wanted to show me.

Oh no, more pictures, I thought. And once again, my guard went up.

"Here, let's sit on the sofa and take a look at them," he said.

The sofa was situated between the bed and the back French doors in the master bedroom. The same bedroom he shared with his wife. I glanced over at the sofa with apprehension. There, strategically sitting on an end table, was a small photo album containing pictures of the Thailand orphanage children.

Why is there a photo album on an end table in the bedroom?

My eyes grew wide as my mind grew suspicious. I scanned the room, noting what appeared to be a preplanned setting. The sofa, the end table, the book—they all seemed ready and waiting for two people to join them. As the moment unfolded, my eyes darted back and forth in an attempt to assess the situation. My hesitancy and confusion must have been obvious, because at that point, Jack broke the silence and began to take charge.

"Amber, have a seat and let me show you the pictures of the children." His tone was kind yet also carried an air of authority.

I reluctantly sat down on the sofa. I was unsure of the situation, and yet there I was, sitting on Jack Hardie's couch, in his bedroom, just a few feet from his bed. *Why* I sat is still a mystery to me. Jack didn't force me. Had I protested and refused, he would not have prevented me from leaving. I wasn't being held hostage. I made a choice to sit on that sofa.

My mind raced with all kinds of thoughts, none of which were good. Uncertain of what he would say next, I decided to break the silence. "Jack, I've seen pictures of the children before."

"But these pictures are different, Amber. And I know how much you love seeing the children." He pulled up a chair, positioning himself directly in front of me, less than a foot away. As he cradled the photo album in his hands, the hairs on his arm just barely touched my arms. I immediately felt my heart rate spike. He continued talking about the pictures, but his eyes were staring straight into mine. I felt my body start to sweat. Jack's hands were now touching mine as we held the book open together. The warmth of his fingers overlapping mine produced an erotic sensation. He scooted forward, inserting his knees between mine as we sat opposite one another. The close proximity of our bodies aroused my unspoken, suppressed feelings for Jack. I knew, without a doubt, that I should immediately stand up and head for the door. But I was frozen, unable to move.

Now mere inches from me, Jack stared into my eyes and spoke softly in his deep, steady voice, "Amber, I have to tell you something."

I didn't want to hear what he had to say.

"Jack, you are making me really nervous."

Our eyes remained fixed on one another.

"There is nothing to be nervous about," he said.

Like a scene out of a frightening dream, I opened my mouth but nothing came out.

When my voice finally returned, I was able to say, "Maybe not. But my heart is pounding out of my chest."

I wanted so badly to stand up and leave, but I remained paralyzed in the moment. Jack stared me in the eyes, his captivating gaze almost hypnotic. He then proceeded to place his hand in the middle of my chest to feel my pounding heart. I had not allowed a man to touch me like this in many years, and the sensation sent shock waves pulsating throughout my body.

I swallowed deeply. My throat was so dry. This was not happening. Surely, at any second, I would wake up in my own bed in a cold sweat. It was too surreal. My inner compass was all over the place, its usual magnetic pull temporarily overpowered by the attraction of something, and some*one*, else.

Our eyes remained locked on one other's and his hand continued holding mine, which was still holding the book. The pounding of my heart was so intense now, I was sure he could hear it.

"Amber?" he spoke softly.

"What…Jack? I said apprehensively.

"I love you."

"I know. You have said that before."

"No, Amber." He paused before continuing. "I mean, I am *in love* with you." And with this declaration, he ever so slowly leaned forward and gently placed his lips on mine.

Instantly, a flash of passion and desire was ignited within me. The photo album fell to the table as he wrapped both his arms securely around me in a full embrace. Like a narcotic, the passion flowing through my veins released a euphoria within. It was an out-of-body experience.

Though still in shock from his kiss, miraculously I was able to muster up the strength to break the magnetic force holding me on that sofa. Jumping to my feet, I placed my hands over my face and began to cry. Taking a deep breath, I turned and began walking toward the back door, trembling the entire way.

Jack quickly came up behind me, wrapping his arms around my shoulders. Pressing his body against me, his embrace tightened. He gently nestled his head close to mine, whispering, "Stop, Amby. Don't go. I'm sorry. I don't know what came over me. My precious Amber Girl, I love you. Please don't leave this way. I never wanted to hurt you. I never will."

We stood there in silence as Jack loosened his grip and put his head on my shoulder.

We both stood in the doorway crying. Every bone in my body was screaming, "Run!" But I stayed, remaining paralyzed and conflicted. His embrace was so comforting. His voice so convincing. He was bigger than life, and I was addicted to his warmth, consumed by his smell, obsessed with his persona. I had fallen for him. I was hooked.

Staring at those French doors, I knew I should leave.

Jack hugged me. "I'm sorry, I'm sorry," he whispered.

I was torn.

"Jack, I really need to go. I really…need…to…go," I whispered.

He tightened his grip on me, nuzzling his head a little closer.

I slowly turned to face him, looking him straight in the eyes, telling him once again that I really had to leave. But Jack was undeterred. Something within me was glad he persisted. The flame inside me was lit and the fire out of control. Wiping the tears from my eyes, he pushed the hair from my face, "Amber, please don't cry."

Staring at him through tear-filled eyes, I tried resisting but the seductive allure was too strong. Our fixed gaze on one another communicated more than words ever could. We stood there in silence, and I felt my body mesmerized by his blue eyes. We kissed, holding each other tightly.

Strangely, it was simultaneously the best *and* worst moment of my life. The exhilarating passion I had always longed for intersecting with the sin I swore I would never, ever commit. Like two unlikely rivers converging, my fulfillment collided with my biggest failure, and that mixed drink proved to be an intoxicating cocktail.

Our lips finally parted. Just when I thought I had reached my shock limit, Jack said something that jolted me to the core.

"Amby, you better leave before I bed you right here and now."

Wait, did he just say that? I thought. *"Bed" me?* But he couldn't be serious about that. Not Jack Hardie. Not my strong Christian coworker who radiated with character and integrity. The man I knew would definitely not say such a thing and mean it.

Jack released me from his manly hug and sat on the sofa, head in his hands, and trying to catch his breath. I stood there still crying in disbelief. I wanted to turn back time. To go back to our earlier phone conversation. To tell him I simply could not meet him in his home. Even with painters there. But that opportunity had come and gone. I had made my choice to come and to stay even when I had the chance to leave. There was no way to unscramble this egg.

Pacing the room, I decided the best thing to do was to come clean concerning my feelings for him. "Okay, let's talk about it, Jack, I love you too, but we…we just can't do this."

I had previously tried denying my feelings for Jack and attempting to bring some sense of reason to them, but they proved too strong. There was now no doubt that we both had feelings for each other, feelings that needed to be harnessed…and right away. Fortunately, Jack had to be at the airport soon to leave for Guatemala. So we agreed to part and call on the phone to talk about what just happened. I exited through the back bedroom door, walked across the lanai, and then through the yard to my car, all the while my body was shaking uncontrollably. I could barely stand on my feet as I ran in high heels back to my car. My black-and-white tailored skirt and black dress shirt felt soaked in sweat. I sat in the car, my head spinning, my heart racing, my body shaking, my spirit grieving.

My mind raced as I tried to avoid a complete meltdown. *How could my life change in an instant? How could I become so blinded to right and wrong? How could I want to do the right thing and then suddenly spiral out of control? How could I get caught in a web of deceit and not know it? Is sin so sly that I ignored all the warning signs? Why? Why?*

Why? Why would a smart person miss such blatant signs of approaching sin? The alarms had been sounding, but for some reason I had been deaf to their warnings. At this point I was totally unaware of the spiritual battle being waged for my heart, soul, and life.

*****

That day became a moment frozen in my history, and one I would never forget. The glimmer in Jack's bright blue eyes and the look on his bewildered face is a picture that would play over and over again in the days and weeks that followed. The kiss was something I would never be able to change. Jack was so handsome, and his charisma so overwhelming and contagious. His presence was all consuming and his polished persona had an uncontrollable power over me.

There was a battle raging in my soul, and it was one I was not prepared to fight. What made matters worse was that I had been so blind to the fact that I had voluntarily placed myself in harm's way. I started the car; and by divine coincidence, the radio, tuned to my favorite Christian station, began playing a Casting Crowns song entitled "Slow Fade," which almost perfectly described the battle I was now facing. It's about fading from black (or white) into grey as the choices we make lead us unknowingly to stray from God.

Driving home, Jack called on his way to the Miami International Airport. We tried to reason away our actions, to rationalize the uncontrolled passion. We attempted to minimize the tsunami of mixed emotions that now flooded our hearts, minds and souls.

Like stepping off a plane into a foreign land, I had entered unknown territory. I was a foreigner to this kind of lifestyle. It seemed I had no guidance or passport. My mind spun. *How does something like this happen to two good people?* But then I wondered, *Or are we?*

Choices

There are defining moments in life that change everything. Some defining moments are beyond our control, such as sickness or death of a loved one. Some of those moments are involuntary. We don't get a vote. They just happen.

However, other defining moments are totally within our control. They are brought into reality by the choices we make and the plans we formulate. Some of those choices end up blessing us while others bring more of a curse. And some decisions we make become like dominoes, affecting the next choice, and the next, and so on.

I had previously decided to sell my home, quit my job, and move to Florida where I would start my life over. Each decision I made was carefully planned. I had thought about it for years. I had diligently prayed, sought wise counsel, researched the possibilities, and cautiously mapped out a plan in preparation for a change in my life's direction. This new venture would be a welcome change filled with excitement and hopeful anticipation for good things to come.

I knew I could change my residence and my career without changing the person I was. The choice to move was a defining part of my life story. I figured if it didn't work out, I could always move back to Massachusetts. No big deal. All the choices I made were painting a living portrait that one day would tell my story. They would give me things to talk about for the rest of my life.

Most planned choices that are not immoral or sinful are nevertheless often hard decisions to ponder. There are no specific guidelines in making these decisions. Instead, they require wisdom and bringing my heart's desire before God. I wanted to make the best decision about where I should live, and though it was a hard decision, I believed it to be the right one for me.

However, there are some defining moments that are the result of poor choices made out of a heart that has drifted from God. Choices that are immoral or sinful *do* have a rulebook to follow with specific guidelines found in the Bible. Those biblical standards were black and white. There was no mistaking them or misunderstanding them. No renegotiation or reinterpretation was necessary. God spoke them in Scripture, and he does not stutter. All I had to do was stay in the white zone and all would be well with my soul. But enter the Grey Zone and I would soon be walking on thin ice. At any time that ice could give way, leading to disaster. I had ignored the cracking beneath my feet for months.

The choices I made leading me into that Grey Zone began changing the very person I wanted to be, altering my character and integrity in slight increments. These choices were rewriting my life story forever. My faith reminded me that with true repentance, I could be forgiven. But the scars my choices brought would remain. I learned that though we are free to choose our sin, there is no freedom of choice in the consequences.

These defining moments are not the stories you want to tell at your class reunion. They are not the legacies you pass on to your children. They are not how you want to be remembered. Sin blinds an intelligent, even spiritual person, from making wise decisions. Sinful decisions muddle the distinct black-and-white lines that are very easy for everyone else to see. Once made, sin can grip a person's mind, creating root systems of twisted thought. Under sin's influence we even believe black is white and white is black. It can take the strongest Christian warrior and turn him/her into a wounded, defeated, prisoner of war in a matter of moments.

Sin makes fools of us all.

Prior to that day at Jack's home, I would have confidently told you, "I would never enter into a relationship with a married man.!" But until we are seduced by sin, we never really know what we are capable of.

So here I was, feeling like I had been unfairly attacked, kidnapped, and dropped into a brutal war zone. However, in reality, I had walked into that battle with both eyes open. The warfare was real and bloody, and I felt powerless to make it stop.

13

What Now?

With Jack now gone to Guatemala, I tried to carry on like nothing had happened. Like life was somehow normal. But it wasn't. I couldn't sleep, eat, or think. It didn't help that Jack called every day from Guatemala on Juanita's satellite phone. I was worried that my number would show up on her phone and that she would begin asking questions. But he just told me I was being overly sensitive and tense. During our conversations, he would ask me if I was okay, if we had damaged our relationship, and if we could go back to normal and begin working together as friends again. He assured me that what happened that day at his house would never happen again. I briefly suggested parting and not working together anymore; but he assured me that we could, and would, get through this mess.

After a week in Guatemala, Jack then flew to Thailand to check on the orphanage children there. He did not call me from Thailand like he had done while in Guatemala. After almost two weeks of silence with no contact, I began to think he was mad at me. I thought our friendship was damaged beyond repair and that perhaps now he was realizing we should no longer be friends. I was confused and didn't know what or how to think.

Upon his return to the states, Jack was aloof. He did not call me right away, and when he did call, his voice was distant. After discussing it further, we agreed, for the sake of the children we were serving, to go on working together. However, I wondered why his demeanor toward me had changed. Was he blaming me for what had happened? Was *I* the one at fault? I already was carrying my own guilt about all this, and now I began wondering if he was condemning me as well. We continued working together via phone calls and e-mails. And for a few weeks Jack's tone remained distant and cold—that is, until Sarah went away again.

About a month after his return from Thailand, Sarah traveled out of state to go see her family again. The day she left town, the phone calls started. He began by asking me to come over to his house in order to finish a project he and I were working on together. It seemed odd to me how comfortable he suddenly was with me coming to his house. I kept thinking that if he was that comfortable with me coming over, then surely, he had everything under control. After the trauma of my last visit, there was no way he would repeat the same mistake twice.

The first night he asked me to come over, I flatly told him no. But the second night he asked, I drove to the house, saw him standing at the door, and then drove away without stopping. I called and explained that I just couldn't bring myself to come in. The third time he asked, he suggested that we talk outside the house. I reasoned that chatting outside would be fine as we could sit on the lanai.

I wanted to see Jack. I needed to talk to him and set all this right and hopefully make sure we could go back to normal. I convinced myself that a good heart-to-heart conversation would help us regain trust and rebuild friendship. So, after reacquainting for a while out on the lanai, we agreed it would be okay to go in the house for a drink of water.

Once inside we conversed about our relationship for hours. We came to an agreement that we could work together for ministry purposes and also maintain a healthy friendship. We were honest about our feelings for each other, but also acknowledged that we were two Christian people who knew right from wrong. We concluded that we could be friends but that there needed to be some strict boundaries.

Jack told me that I was the friend he always dreamed he would have in Sarah. She had little interest in his ministry projects and that left him feeling very alone. He told me how much he enjoyed talking with me and how he loved my younger perspective and insight. Then he confessed that he and Sarah rarely even spoke to one another, and that they lived very separate lives. That explained why Sarah went away alone and why Jack went on mission trips.

Further, he said he believed we could continue working together and serving the ministries that were depending on us. "Amber, I love having a companion who genuinely has a heart for missions like you. Sarah has never helped me with any of my mission projects."

I felt humbled and honored to help with his international projects. It made me beam with joy. I responded, telling him how much I loved having a man in my life.

"Jack, you have to understand that I have never had anyone I could really talk to or trust with my problems. That's why I so appreciate your advice and insight."

We made such an effective team for the ministry, it didn't make sense to discontinue that work. Considering how many lives would be affected should we disband, I wanted him to know I would continue our working relationship for the good of all involved. Jack was encouraged to hear that and said he was thrilled to be friends.

Our talk that evening yielded some positive steps moving forward, and we reached a mutual agreement regarding boundaries and restrictions. We were both ecstatic and relieved that we were able to work it out and still maintain a healthy friendship. Enjoying our newfound relationship, and being blinded by our inappropriate intimacy, we continued to talk until the magnetic force became so strong that there was no walking away. I was in uncharted waters, slowly getting sucked right into the middle of a whirlpool.

We talked on into the evening, as the grandfather clock in the entryway chimed hour after hour after hour. Jack wanted me to stay even later, but I knew I had to go as it was now the wee hours of the morning. Jack promised he would never "force himself" on me, and yet I knew his gentleness could also be a powerful and persuasive force as well.

I left that evening, only to return the next day, where I again heard the hourly chime of that grandfather clock over and over and over again. Jack had awoken something inside of me that had been dead for so long. The "Do Not Disturb" sign that once hung on my forehead was battered and broken and now swinging adrift in a wild sea of emotions.

My shades of grey grew darker, and before long, Jack and I both admitted we had fallen in love with each other.

14

Walking in Darkness

When the smoke cleared and our emotions settled a bit, Jack and I agreed it would not be a good idea for us to continue meeting in private. We needed to stay apart before we eventually lost all control. We began speaking on the phone for hours at a time, sending countless e-mails back and forth, and continuing to work together for the good of the charities we were serving.

However, we agreed to keep our relationship under control while Jack pursued a divorce from Sarah, which he insisted was long overdue. By this time his charisma and charm had totally consumed me, and I was captivated by his fascination toward me. We occasionally met at local restaurants for lunch, reasoning that if we were out in public, it would be okay. If anyone saw us together, it could easily be justified as two coworkers enjoying a friendly lunch.

It was during this time that I learned about Jack's unfair, cruel, and difficult childhood, growing up on the outskirts of Houston, Texas. As a very young child, he was abused by his stepfather and often watched helplessly as his stepfather brutally beat his mother. He had no one in his life to go to for help as his father had died in the war. He was poor and all alone, a small child walking the streets looking for other families to feed him and show him love. Hanging out with the older neighborhood boys, Jack heard and saw a lot of inappropriate behavior.

At a young age he had to find work in order to put food on the family table. He took a job in a local gas station, where he proved himself a hard worker. The owner of the gas station, Mr. Johnson, really liked Jack and took him under his wing. Mr. Johnson had also grown up in a poor family, but he had become quite successful thanks to a loving uncle. Now he was determined to do the same for Jack, and he began mentoring him. He also helped Jack's mother and his family by bringing them food and helping them pay rent. Jack was especially fond of Mr. Johnson and grateful for his generosity and kindness.

Hearing Jack's life story, I was shocked. Revealing his emotional childhood stories, something he never did with anyone, made me feel honored he could trust me with such deep and painful memories. He cried, and I held him tight to comfort him.

Being a former Marine, Mr. Johnson encouraged Jack to join the Marines to further his education. Jack did exactly as Mr. Johnson suggested, eventually completing his education while serving his country. Growing up, Jack was often teased for his raggedy clothes. He never had anyone in his life who encouraged him, so he just goofed off in school, often getting into trouble. But after joining the service and starting his education, the Marines helped him to tap into his true potential. He had just never been given the encouragement he needed to succeed, and once he was properly motivated, he began to excel. Jack began to have real dreams of starting his own business upon finishing his tour of duty.

Returning home from the service, he met Sarah at a party and shortly thereafter they were married, mostly for companionship. Jack didn't like to be alone. When Mr. Johnson realized Jack had returned home and gotten married, he was only too happy to reemploy his best worker and friend. Having no children of his own, he treated Jack like a son, teaching him everything he knew. And of course, having no father, Jack bonded with Mr. Johnson and absorbed all he had to teach. The two of them were an inseparable pair. And due in part to Jack's hard work ethic, he helped Mr. Johnson build a very successful business.

Unfortunately, Mr. Johnson died very suddenly of a heart attack one day at work, and Jack was unable to save him. Jack was devastated at his loss and swore he would carry on Mr. Johnson's legacy. This surrogate father was the most generous, caring man Jack knew. Mr. Johnson had been determined to make the world a better place, and Jack was determined to carry on that dream for him. Over the years he worked his way up the ladder of success, eventually ending up in the oil industry where he made his fortune. He was a strong-willed independent young man who had persevered through life, never being truly happy, but always doing his best to make others happy.

Jack was a true survivor. And people like that usually choose either one of two paths. Some survivors wallow in their desperation, causing them to never get anywhere in life. They habitually blame others for their despondent situation and lack of advancement. They may end up with addictive personalities, seeking drugs or alcohol to soothe the pain.

Other survivors choose the path of extreme confidence. They believe they are going to conquer the world, no matter what. They are determined to forge their own destinies and affect the future of their descendants and of the people with whom they come in contact. They transform their own misfortunes into fuel for helping others.

That was Jack Hardie's story. He was single-minded about making the world a better place for his family, friends, the ministries he served, and the people God brought into his life. Jack received his joy through helping others, just like how Mr. Johnson had once helped him.

Years into their marriage Sarah and Jack began attending a church where Jack discovered a passion and excitement for mission trips. However, according to Jack, he truly never loved his wife, therefore these mission adventures were his excuse to get away from what he perceived as the misery of a loveless marriage. So he traveled the world, generously giving away his wealth to help those in need.

And yet he claimed he never felt appreciated by his "nagging wife." Therefore, helping homeless, poor people and children around the world was how he filled that void of satisfaction in his life. He confessed to me that he was now officially done with living a lie and was relieved to finally be divorcing his wife. He even made the divorce sound selfless, saying it was not fair for Sarah to live in such a loveless marriage.

But out of all the mission endeavors Jack pioneered and led, his project in Thailand was his favorite. At least six times a year, he traveled there to check on the children at the orphanage. During this intensified season of "getting to know each other better," Jack opened up to me about a lot of personal issues. I learned from him there was a woman in Thailand that had become his good friend. Her name was Nyri. He assured me they were just good friends, but he would visit with her each time he was there. He described her as a "sweet young lady" working for a Christian organization in Thailand. He took her out to fine restaurants while he was there on mission trips but promised me nothing sexually inappropriate ever occurred between them.

Jack held nothing back and wanted me to know everything about him. He also said he wanted to come clean about his life and that there would be no secrets between us like he had with Sarah. He wanted us to start over with a clean slate.

"Amby, I love you so much. And now that we have found each other and fallen in love, we can finally have the life we've both always wanted."

All of this seemed fair to me. There was even a sense of moral justice to it. Sarah would be freed from a miserable marriage and taken care of financially. Jack would stop living a lie, and I would finally have the man and marriage I had longed for all my life. I was beyond flattered that Jack loved and trusted me enough to share his secrets. He also gave me his word he would not contact Nyri anymore, and if she contacted him in some way, he would let me know. That made sense to me, and I believed him. I was thrilled with the prospect of the open communication we were developing since I had never experienced that type of honesty in my entire twenty years of marriage.

The more Jack disclosed to me, the more I felt sad for the lack of love he was experiencing in his marriage. I believed him when he said he was always searching for love, a love he had now found in me. And with our newfound open line of communication, I began letting him know how much I loved him too. However, I made it clear that I wasn't going to be the "other woman" and the reason for his divorce from Sarah. Jack reassured me that I was not the reason for the decision to leave his marriage.

I also did not want to be intimate with Jack while he was still married to Sarah, and Jack said he understood. However, he continually tried charming me into intimate encounters. I tried to explain to Jack the turmoil I was feeling in my heart for entering into this kind of relationship with him. Yet whenever I tried to back away, I ended up wavering in my own desires for his love, friendship, and affection.

Not long after learning about his friendship with Nyri and as I was still trying to curtail our level of intimacy, Jack told me of yet another female friend of his. This story was a bit more difficult for me to digest. Chen was a poor, young, handicapped girl from Thailand that he had met in the marketplace. He related how her warm smile and big heart melted his own and that he felt compelled to help her. He began by researching medical options to see if anything could be done to remedy her handicap. Next, he purchased her a car and then a home in Thailand. Somewhere in the midst of that relationship, Jack said he believed they fell in love with one another. He then admitted to me that his frequent visits to Thailand involved more than just caring for the orphanage. He and Chen had actually set up a house together.

In time it also became apparent that the ministry e-mail address Jack wanted me to use for e-mailing him was not an e-mail address for "business" after all. He had set up this particular e-mail address so the women from Thailand could correspond with him without Sarah knowing. Giving the e-mail address a "business" name would also keep Nyri and Chen from knowing how sly he was acting. I suddenly realized I had fallen for the same story. I had been e-mailing him on the "business" e-mail for well over a year, never knowing it was an e-mail account for his "women."

Did I suspect anything? I had every reason to trust him. In truth, I was totally blind to his lack of honesty in our own relationship. For the last two years I had come up with all kinds of reasons to excuse his overly friendly innuendos toward me. It never occurred to me that this was his lifestyle and I was just one of several women who received his charm and affection.

As I thought through these stories, it became clear why he had become somewhat distant after his last trip to Thailand. He was there with someone else. I remembered how he had called me every day from Guatemala but the phone calls abruptly stopped once he got to Thailand. I concluded he was torn between the relationships he had on the other side of the world and the emotions he had started with me in his own town.

All of these new revelations were way too much for me to handle, and this prompted me to back away from our relationship as I processed his motives and actions. However, I was so desperately smitten by this man's interest in me and my emotions for him that it made it hard for me to make rational and good choices concerning him.

But the least I could do would be to curtail our intimacy while I contemplated my situation and his sincerity toward me. As I attempted to move toward a healthier relationship with Jack, he began revealing more and more of his previous plans for Chen and his ministry in Thailand. He had decided to divorce Sarah, then return to Thailand and marry Chen. Of course, Chen swallowed his proposal hook, line and sinker. Jack then told me he and Chen had plans to open a special orphanage for handicapped children in Thailand and that once completed, he would leave Sarah and never return to the States.

"I was going to divorce Sarah from a distance as she is a good woman at heart and because I couldn't bear to see her in pain. But it wouldn't be fair to Sarah for us to continue being together since I have never loved her," Jack said.

This new information was difficult to hear, and it yet made me feel sympathetic toward Jack's sad life. If anyone could identify with what it's like to be in a troubled marriage, it was me. I fully understood it was something that was not easy to endure. Any man willing to consider this type of "escape plan" concerning his marriage must be pretty miserable. The more I sympathized with Jack, the more he told me, and the more I let my guard down. However, I continued to maintain distance regarding our intimacy.

Jack also shared with me that he had convinced Sarah he was impotent, just so she wouldn't "bother" him in the bedroom. He said he simply didn't have any romantic or sexual feelings for Sarah and for those reasons found it virtually impossible to make love to her. Convincing Sarah of his impotence freed up Jack's conscience, enabling him to justify his indiscretions and the move he was about to make to Thailand to be with Chen. All this, he said, was derailed when he fell in love with me.

In me, he explained, he discovered a love he didn't know existed and a passion he had never experienced. He now realized his love for Chen was based more on pity, not real love. He began the relationship feeling sorry for her, and their feelings developed into caring for one another.

"I really thought it was love, Amber," he confessed during one of our heartfelt sessions. "But I was wrong. Because I never really loved Sarah and was never happy I unconsciously was always searching for love. That is, until now...until *you*."

The more I listened to him bear his soul, the more I felt honored to have his love. I believed Jack and every word of his story, just like Nyri and Chen had done.

I felt flattered too that he trusted me enough to come clean with me about his illicit life overseas. He made me feel special in telling me secrets he could never have told his own wife, especially about his indiscretions. Jack now wanted a clean slate and a fresh start—no more secrets and no more lies. He promised to tell me everything going forward. He swore he would never return to Thailand, even though he had previously promised the two of us would visit the orphanage one day. I believed him when he said he wouldn't return there, and such a promise would be easily verified as he couldn't well sneak clear across the world without me knowing it. So I figured he was telling the truth. Any man who loved me enough to trust me with the most intimate details of his troubled, lonely, loveless life, surely wouldn't lie to me about traveling internationally. Or was I so far into the grey that I was no longer able to tell the difference between the truth and lies?

I did take some comfort in Jack's assertion that he had already planned to divorce his wife long before he fell in love with me. He assured me their problems were not my fault, but that he was determined to see the divorce go through. He convinced me that once he was free from his marriage to Sarah, he would then properly court me "like a decent man should."

He then strangely added that if I were to back out of our relationship, he would leave the country and go to Thailand to be with Chen. He reasoned that this would be better than staying in his loveless, depressing marriage.

I now was convinced I was not the "other woman." Rather than being the villain, I was more akin to a heroine in his story. I was the friend that saved Jack from a grave mistake with the *real* "other woman" in Thailand. I had rescued him from leaving the country for all the wrong reasons.

Believe it or not, in the charcoal darkness of this relationship, it all seemed right. It felt like love.

15

Juanita

Jack and I tried staying apart as best we could. However, being so engrossed in ministry projects around the world, being away from each other proved next to impossible. We kept in contact via e-mail, phone conversations, and occasional lunches together, which were always in public places. I still saw Jack (and Sarah) in church and at their Bible study meetings, though attending made me feel extremely uncomfortable. I expressed this concern to Jack; however, he convinced me everything should remain as normal while he pursued his divorce. He repeatedly assured me that everything would be fine in time.

As I entered Jack's home for the first time since admittedly falling in love with him, my heart was both convicted and anguished. I was privately tormented by the fact that Jack had such control over me that he could convince me something like this would be okay. It was as if two people were living inside me.

That evening while Jack was standing and teaching the crowd, I was sitting on the couch when I heard the familiar sound of the grandfather clock chime in the dining room. Every chime seemed to reverberate throughout the entire house. Jack glanced over at me and smiled like a child who had just stolen a cookie and gotten away with it. I just looked down at my open Bible in silence, knowing he was thinking the same thing I was. The chimes reminded us both of our long evenings together. The echo of each chime called to mind our many surreptitious evenings together.

My heart pounded, and I began sweating, my dulled conscience trying its best to conceal my hideous secret. At this stage my guilt had become unbearable, and yet our situation did not seem to bother Jack at all. He never missed a beat as he continued his biblical teaching, periodically smiling and glancing my way. While I could hardly bear the inward shame, Jack actually seemed amused by the clock's ringing and the dark secret we held together. That night was the last time I ever went to Jack's home for Bible study.

Months passed, and in November, Jack hosted a fundraiser for the Guatemalan orphanage. That's when I met Juanita for the first time. Juanita was the president and founder of the orphanage Jack helped to sponsor. Jack had verbally portrayed her as a "tomboy" who was a bit crazy for trekking in Guatemalan mountains with very few supplies. The pictures Jack took three months prior, while there on the mission field with her, confirmed his "crazy tomboy" description. However, now meeting Juanita in person at this fundraiser dinner, in a country club setting, allowed me to see her through another lens altogether.

That evening I encountered the Guatemalan-American woman. Unlike the rough outdoorsy woman I expected, Juanita was very pretty with long black velvet-colored hair and a small, slender body. Though in her forties, she had never married. She was a woman on a mission for God's kingdom, filled with confidence and determined to make a difference in the world for Him.

I remember feeling a bit jealous of Juanita and her ministry involvement with Jack. It felt strange for me to be envious of this woman, especially since I knew in my heart Jack was not rightfully mine, at least not *yet*.

All the drama and trauma of the last several months led me to a crossroads in my life. After considering my options, I made the difficult decision to quit my job at WeCareWorld and get a regular job outside of ministry. I needed space between myself and Colby, as the guilt I was carrying became unbearable. Every time I saw Colby and whenever he spoke of Jack, I was pointedly reminded of my sin. Colby believed Jack to be his best friend, but I knew better. I knew Colby really didn't know Jack at all. And I could no longer get up every day and be reminded of the sin and charade I was living.

Eventually, I landed a secular accounting job that offered a much higher salary. This made it much easier when I explained why I was leaving the company to Colby. I knew he couldn't pay me competitively compared to a non-ministry firm. In typical Colby fashion, he was gracious and wished me well and we parted our working relationship on good terms. I saw this as a blessing in light of what could have happened had Colby discovered my real relationship with Jack. So I was thankful for this amicable separation from the ministry as I searched for any silver lining to the cloud I was under at the time. Shortly after I resigned from WeCareWorld, Jack also resigned from the board of directors and some of his other church positions, saying he was much too busy to split himself between so many ministries.

Christmastime came, and Jack and I had planned to carve out time to enjoy a nice Christmas lunch together and to exchange presents. Jack bought me a beautiful, rather pricey, gold-and-diamond necklace, which I loved. What he did not count on was that the jewelry store would send him a thank-you note for his extravagant purchase. Giving his real name and address to them was not the smartest move, but then again neither were most of his other actions.

As fate would have it, Sarah opened the mail and discovered the truth. She questioned him about the purchase, and Jack admitted to purchasing a nice present for me. But the way he spun his response was classic Jack Hardie, explaining to her that the gift was out of gratitude for all my hard work and how I had faithfully supported his mission projects on a voluntary basis.

"In light of all she has done for me, it was the least I could do for Amber," he explained.

Sarah nevertheless was rightfully upset that I had accepted a very expensive and inappropriate gift. Even so, she accepted his explanation. Jack could convince Sarah to believe anything.

On New Year's Eve, we both attended a party. I went alone and sat at a table with friends while Jack sat at another table with Sarah. It was getting much harder to hide our feelings, and yet we were determined to pretend as if everything was still the same in our friendship. My twisted perspective and torn heart continued pumping the pain of guilt throughout my spirit. I was walking with one foot securely planted on the path of sin while the other continued the outward walk of a dedicated Christian.

Though Sarah remained sweet and kind, I could tell she was looking at me a little differently. Before the night was over, Sarah walked right up to me, smiling.

"Hi, Amber. I haven't seen you in a while. How is your new job?"

The weight of my double life was becoming too hard to bear. I was living out the reality of the Proverb, "Good judgment wins favor, but the way of the unfaithful leads to their destruction."[3] Deception and guilt were choking the life out of my heart and soul.

"The job is going well, although I miss working with Colby and helping the ministries through WeCareWorld. Colby was a great boss," I said. I wanted to fill the air with meaningless chitchat to divert Sarah's attention from the gift Jack had given me.

"Yes, that's what Jack says. Jack misses working with that ministry too. Colby had to be the best boss ever. He is always so much fun," Sarah said.

Though Sarah seemed sincere about her kindness toward me, I was still waiting for her to bring up the dreaded necklace. I continued rambling in an attempt to prevent Sarah from talking.

"I am sure God has a plan for WeCareWorld Ministries and will supply Colby with another accountant soon," I said.

Sarah nodded in agreement, "Yes, God always has a plan."

---

[3] Proverbs 13:15

I scanned the room, hoping Jack would come rescue me from the awkwardness of the conversation, but he didn't. He remained seated quietly at his table by himself. Looking down at the floor, I agreed, "Yes, God always has a plan."

Fortunately, Sarah did not bring up the necklace, and within minutes our conversation was over. I quickly made my way back to my table and sat with friends.

Sarah returned to sit with Jack, who sat quietly, waiting for her return, all the while peering over his glasses in our direction. It was almost as if he actually enjoyed watching our encounter and the potential drama unfold.

Seeing Sarah that night was an excruciating experience in my heart, mind, and soul. By all accounts she seemed to be such a kind woman, a far cry from the picture Jack had painted of her. I had difficulty imagining the harsh stories he had told me. However, it was clear he was not happy when he was with her, and I watched him restlessly squirm through the group games they played that evening.

Sarah and Jack left early from the party, before the clock struck midnight. I also left early, went home, and cried myself to sleep. My tears flowed partly because I missed Jack, but mostly because of my shame. My secret was tearing me apart from the inside out. That night was the last time I ever saw Sarah.

*****

My relationship with Jack continued moving forward, and before long, we weren't just having public lunches, I was also allowing Jack to visit me at my home. Soon, he became a fixture in my neighborhood, speaking to all my neighbors. He would park his car right in front of my house. He helped me with household chores, and even assisted me when I painted and redesigned my entire lanai. He didn't attempt to hide his presence there at my house and was extremely brazen. He was also quick to justify it.

"Amber girl, everyone is going to find out sooner or later about our relationship, so what different does it make?"

I, on the other hand, was constantly warning him to be cautious, but with little success. Everyone knew we worked together on ministry projects and that we were friends, so when people saw us together, they just continued assuming we were good friends. But in time that perception would change.

16

Protection

One day, Jack came over to the house with his usual bouquet of fresh flowers. Only this time he also brought an unusual gift.

"Okay, Amby, in this box is a special present. I know this is going to be quite different than most of my presents, but I really want you to have this," he said. His face was fixed on me with a look of great anticipation.

I could not imagine what could be causing this kind of exhilaration. I loved his presents as they were always very carefully thought out.

"I can't wait to open it," I exclaimed.

"Now don't be frightened," Jack said cautiously.

"What? Frightened?" I was confused. "Why would your present *frighten* me?"

Opening the box, I first spotted bullets; and then, looking further, I saw a shiny, silver-and-brown Smith & Wesson handgun. I was not accustomed to guns and had never owned one. I pulled it out and held it at a distance while it dangled from my finger.

"Okay, this is different," I said, laughing. "How kind of you."

"Now, Amber, I know this is an odd present. But I am genuinely concerned about you. I can't stand the thought of you being all alone in this house. I want you to be able to protect yourself, until I am able to be here to protect you. So please humor me, accept this gift, and let me teach you how to use it."

Now that's sweet. Even if I had never handled a handgun before, the thought behind his caring actions was more than I had ever experienced. His loving concern far exceeded that of any other man. No one had ever treated me like Jack Hardie had. He was always so thoughtful, loving, kind, and generous. He always seemed to want the best for me.

"Oh, Jack. You're unbelievable. I cannot believe the way you care for me. Thank you." I placed the gun on the table and gave him a hug. My heart was filled with gratitude for his deep concern. And he responded, returning my embrace, encircling me in his arms. This brought me to tears.

Jack took the gun out of the case and spent the afternoon teaching me to load, unload, and shoot it. His loving-kindness was captivating, and I felt safe and secure under his full control.

Our times together were precious and getting more and more frequent. Jack made up a few additional excuses to carve out extra time together. He told Sarah he was playing a lot of golf, running errands, or just going for a ride on the Harley.

But having Jack around all the time didn't make it easy when it came to our physical feelings for one another. I made it very clear to him that although I had entered into this relationship with him, I was adamant that we be married before consummating our relationship. When the time was right, I explained that I "wanted it all." And that would only happen after he was divorced. Then we could be together. I told him I wanted a small wedding with family and friends only and that I wanted to consummate our relationship on our wedding night. Jack promised to honor my wishes. But the blindness caused by sin and emotional infatuation with Jack made me unbelievably stupid.

I did my best to abstain from intimacy for as long as I could, but eventually, I became powerless under his spell and gave in to Jack's advances. We were crazy in love and inseparable as a couple, spending as much time as we could steal away together. Jack promised me his divorce was imminent, and I believed him with all my heart.

What once was grey became straight-up black, and I no longer cared. This was now my new normal. I had willingly and knowingly compromised our relationship, my future, and all that had once been important to me. There was no more wanting and waiting to "have it all." I was now getting what I wanted and a good bit more than I had bargained for.

At the time Jack seemed like the perfect love for me. As a matter of fact I even called him Mr. Wonderful. Our favorite song was "Can't Help Falling in Love with You" by Andrea Bocelli. The words just seemed to exactly fit our exact situation, and Jack sang it to me every time we were together. He would put on the song, and then his deep, seductive voice would fill the room as he sang about wise men and fools rushing in and a love that was meant to be. Both of us believed that ours was indeed a love that was "meant to be."

Jack's voice captivated my heart as he had total power and control over me. He continually sang songs to me from his era, and I loved hearing them. He knew how much I loved flowers and kept the vase on my dining room table filled with fresh-smelling, beautiful flowers day after day. As soon as the flowers began to wilt, he would bring a new bouquet. I constantly warned him about running into people he knew at the florist, but he didn't seem to care.

"Don't be so paranoid," he would say.

*****

One day Jack showed up with his usual bouquet of flowers, but with them he also brought long white PVC pipes, bolts, locks, and a grin from ear to ear. Opening the door, I stood there with disbelief and confusion on my face. My voice was steady but slow as I processed the view before me.

"Okay, Jack, now what are you doing?" I asked.

"Well, I didn't tell you ahead of time because I knew you would object," he said, determined and confident. Then clearing his throat and looking over to the sliding glass doors leading out to the lanai, he said, "I want to secure your front and back doors." Jack stood there with a big smile, holding the long white PVC pole and packages of locks and bolts. He waited apprehensively for me to respond to his quirky behavior.

I hesitated for a moment, processing his new request. There was a part of me that wanted to laugh at his silly actions. However, I also wanted to cry over his deep concern for me. I never had anyone so kind in my life. It felt so good to have a protector, a friend, a love. My heart flooded with deep appreciation and a love I never experienced in my life.

I exploded with enthusiasm. "Oh, Jack, you are so wonderful."

Jack needed to hear words of affirmation more than I needed the locks.

"How do you come up with this stuff?" My eyes began to tear up as I contemplated his thoughtful and caring spirit. Jack looked at me with adoration.

"It's easy, Amber. I love you. Love is what you do, not what you say. I am so worried about you all the time. I just want to be able to protect you while we are apart." Jack too began to tear up as he watched me melt with appreciation. He quickly wiped his tears away and then began taking control of the situation. "I'll feel so much better when we are together, and I can protect you."

My heart overflowed with happiness. How could I possibly say no to his request? At times I felt guilty that he served me this way. I was certainly not accustomed to someone taking care of my every need like this. Not to mention to meet needs I didn't even know I had. Wrapping my arms around him, I gave him a kiss.

"What can I say, Jack? You are amazing. You do not have to always dream up ways to serve me, Jack. I love you just the way you are."

Jack pushed my curls away from my face as his bright blue eyes peered into mine. He smiled. Returning the embrace, his deep voice whispered into my ear. "I know you do, Amby. You are putting up with me through a very difficult time." He squeezed a little harder, rubbing my back. Then, pulling away, he took hold of both my shoulders with his hands and looked me in the eyes. "However, I love you and I will do anything it takes to prove that." His caring words steadied my heart and soul like an anchor to a ship, forming a bond in our relationship that was growing stronger.

Jack spent the rest of the day putting extra bolts on the doors, securing the sliding glass door with locks and a long PVC pole, installing a house alarm, putting dimmer switches on the outlets, and fixing plumbing issues. He watched me as I cooked, and I looked on as he worked around the house. We made a great team, and our love and compassion for each other was all consuming. I was so used to dealing with household issues on my own, and having Jack around made me feel complete. Though my future was uncertain, I believed that, with Jack, everything would be okay.

17

Acts of Kindness

Jack arrived at my home one afternoon, carrying two bags as he walked in the front door.

"What's this?" I asked.

He set the bags down and gave me a warm embrace and a passionate kiss. "Oh, just some things I know you need," Jack said, grinning.

"Really, Jack?" I couldn't imagine what I possibly needed that would be important enough for him to buy me on his way over for lunch.

Jack could not contain his excitement. "Go ahead and reach into the bag." As I looked inside the bag, his smile grew. He was like a child on Christmas morning.

"Why are *you* so excited?" I asked, laughing. "I thought these gifts were for *me*."

"They are, Amber. But I just love buying you gifts and watching your face as you open them."

His kindness was so endearing, and his gentle spirit was all consuming. This was part of what made his love so addicting. Inside the bag I discovered a set of butcher-block kitchen knives, a wood-cutting board, wine glasses, a small high-beam flashlight, a mega bundle of AA batteries, and a Mont Blanc pen.

As I unpacked the bag, I laughed, surprised at such an odd arrangement of gifts.

"You see, Amber, I have observed how you cut a tomato." He reached over to grab a nearby tomato sitting on the counter. "When you cut a tomato, you hold it in your hand and cut it with the knife going toward your fingers." He motioned toward his fingers as he spoke. "If you do that, you're going to get hurt one day. You're supposed to place the tomato on a cutting board." He picked up the wood-cutting board, placed it on the counter, and positioned the tomato on top. "You needed a butcher-block cutting board." He smiled as he began to demonstrate the positioning of the tomato on the cutting board.

I was in awe of his impromptu demonstration.

"In order to do this properly, you also needed a new set of sharper kitchen knives." He picked up one of the newly-purchased knives from the counter, holding it in his hand. "A knife should slide easily through the skin of the tomato." Jack began showing off his cutting skills with the sharp knife by easily slicing the tomato into thin, even slices. "See? Your old knives can't do this. They're not very sharp, and I am afraid you will get cut."

My heart was touched by Jack's sensitivity and thoughtfulness.

Jack looked down at the array of gifts, picking up two different-sized wine glasses. He then began teaching a lesson on wine glasses, holding them up to demonstrate their differences. "I got these wine glasses because you appear to only have one set, and we are using the same glasses for both red and white wine." He winked.

Jack was always supplying me with useful bits of information.

"White wine should be in the smaller wine glasses, and the red wine should be in the larger rounded wine glasses. I want to be sure you have enough when you have friends over." He then reached over, picked up the flashlight, and turned it on. "I got you this flashlight so you can see in the dark and not shoot yourself in the foot," he said, laughing.

Jack turned off the flashlight and placed it on the counter. He then picked up the bundle of batteries. "Now this gift is a necessity. You can never have enough of these." he said. "I got you the mega bundle of AA batteries because your TV remote doesn't work." He looked over at the TV, alluding to our last movie together when we discovered the remote was dead. "Now you will never run out of batteries for your TV remote, the flashlight, or anything else that needs batteries." The wide smile on my face was merely a representation of what my heart and soul were feeling.

Then Jack reached for an elegant and expensive Mont Blanc pen. "Now this gift, my dear, is special," he explained, holding it up and turning it in all directions for me to see. "This pen is made quite well." His eyes met mine as he grinned. "This pen will write smooth and clean. However, the best part is that I doubt you will be able to break the clip on this one."

We both cracked up, remembering earlier times when Jack made me so nervous that I broke off my pen clips. I reached up for Jack's hand, wrapping my fingers around it as he held the pen. I gazed up at him. "I doubt I will break it now that I won't be fidgeting with the clip."

Jack leaned down to kiss me.

His perception of my needs brought an enormous sense of fun and security to my relationship with him. Even if they didn't seem like urgent needs to me, I was nevertheless clearly smitten by his ability to observe my life and respond by supplying me with such presents.

"Thank you so much, Jack," I said. "No one has ever cared for me the way you do. I know this isn't right, but I love you so much."

There was no doubt about it. I had fallen deeply in love with this married man. I knew it was wrong, and yet I still genuinely believed we were meant for each other and destined to be together. I sincerely believed God had used me to save Jack from a horrible mistake of leaving the country to be with Chen. Having Jack for myself was a "reward," and I believed I was his, sent to help him straighten out his life. And further confirmation of this was that we would soon be together and everything would be okay.

Jack grabbed me, holding me tight in his arms. "No, thank *you*, my love, for your great sense of appreciation…even if for such little things like these." He then paused, as if contemplating. He then said, "C. S. Lewis wrote something that reminds me so much of you, my sweet Amber. 'Small acts of kindness and remembrance are those that strike deepest to the caring heart.' And you, my love, are a caring heart." He began to silently cry, whispering in my ear, "I love you more, Amber. I love you more."

18

Slowly Dying with a Smile

I knew I could ask Jack for anything and he wouldn't hesitate to get it for me. Even so, I never asked him for a single thing. I didn't want him to think my love for him was based on his generosity. There were times Jack would tell me ahead of time what he was going to buy for me, and I would ask him not to purchase it. I was already having a hard enough time explaining my new gifts to family members.

We spent as much time together as we could. Jack would either bring lunch over to my house or come and help me cook. He always helped clean up (something I loved about him) or even tell me to sit and relax while he graciously cleaned and we chatted about the day.

We both loved the ways we were so much alike. We were both organized, clean, and liked having everything in order. We began sharing routine daily tasks together. Over time I could finish Jack's sentences and he could tell what I was thinking. But though we were both perfectionists, ironically, we were blind to the fact that both our lives were in complete disarray.

*****

One weekend Jack showed up carrying paint buckets and brushes. I just stared at him from the front door with an inquisitive, playful frown on my face.

"*Now* what are you planning, Jack?"

"Well, you said you wanted to redo your lanai, right?" Setting all his supplies on the floor, he looked at me with great expectation. "Amby, by the end of the weekend, I am going to transform your lanai into a restful retreat."

I just shook my head. "Jack, you don't have to do this. We can just relax for the weekend."

Jack promptly picked up the paint cans. "And pass up on all this weekend fun? Not a chance!" He smiled as he walked the supplies out to the lanai.

We spent the entire weekend repainting my lanai in dark brown and soft tan and grey colors. However, on Saturday, while in the middle of the painting, the doorbell rang. It was my parents, very *un*-expectantly stopping by to say hi. I panicked, not knowing what to do. However, Jack stayed cool as a cucumber, telling me not to worry.

"Don't worry. There's nothing we can do about it, so just let them in and remain calm," he reassured me.

Of course, my parents already knew who Jack was. Since they knew him to be kind, they thought nothing of his generosity in helping me with such a big project. The four of us sat around and chatted for a while, and before leaving, Mom and Dad thanked Jack for being so helpful to their daughter.

When they finally drove out of the driveway, I plopped back on the sofa, wiping the sweat from my brow. Jack joined me, placing an arm around my shoulder.

"Amber, don't be nervous. They didn't suspect a thing."

He pushed my curly dark hair away from my face, revealing my big brown eyes. "Even if they did suspect something, it really doesn't matter, does it?"

I looked at him, confused and speechless.

"Listen, Amber, they are going to find out about us someday. We are not going to be able to hide our love forever. If it is sooner than later, so be it."

Leaning back on that couch, his calm voice was like a blanket of comfort. It was also very convincing. Jack hugged me in a full embrace as a million thoughts raced through my head.

Later that day, and to my utter surprise, Jack had all-new patio furniture delivered to my house. We spent the afternoon arranging the new furniture and hanging décor on the lanai walls. Then Jack ran back to the store for pots and plants to complete the design. We both worked feverishly side by side all weekend to finish the project while Sarah was out of town. We ceaselessly complimented each other's abilities, Jack saying he was not used to getting so much help on a household project and me letting him know I wasn't used to anyone doing such wonderful things for me. That evening, when the whole project was finally completed, we sat in the newly decorated lanai, complete with candles, wine, and Jack's favorite music playing. We loved relaxing and dreaming about what the future would bring.

*****

The following Sunday morning, I returned home from church to find Jack proudly sitting on the newly painted lanai, waiting for me. I could see him smiling as I pulled up.

"Jack, what are you doing here?" I asked.

"Well, you needed shelves in your garage, so I figured I would install them for you."

My garage was already clean and hardly had anything in it. The few items I did have in there were sitting on the floor. Apparently, though, Jack thought I needed shelves, which he installed as a surprise for me. He seemed so proud of his accomplishment.

"I took the items that were on the floor and placed them in their proper departments on the shelves. So now you have a section for garden supplies, paint supplies, beach paraphernalia, and car necessities," he said, smiling and visibly proud of his accomplishment. "Oh, and I also bought you a tool box and filled it with all the tools you need if something should happen around here."

Tears began to well up in my eyes as I reflected on his kindness. "Oh, Jack, you are the most wonderful man in the world," I said in a soft voice.

He grinned back at me with such contentment. Having been deprived of words of affirmation for so long, he loved hearing my encouragement and gratitude.

"Oh, and one other thing," he added, "I also picked up a leaf blower, so you can easily clean off the newly decorated lanai in a few minutes." He was beaming, and his bright blue eyes melted my heart. "By the way, where were you?" he asked suddenly. The tone in his voice had changed.

I hesitated to answer. Jack had already resigned from all the ministries he was representing. Further, he had also resigned his church membership so that no one would have the "right" to confront him concerning his actions. I, on the other hand, still chose to make an occasional church appearance (against Jack's wishes) to ward off any potential suspicions.

I was so sorry for the life I was leading but believed it to be a temporary situation. I knew that everything would work out right eventually. In the meantime I would maintain my good reputation while we both waited for Jack's divorce.

"I went to church," I answered sheepishly. I could immediately see the look of disapproval on Jack's face, though he would never say anything out loud.

Since my son was still the church's worship leader, I was torn between the mother and Christian I once was and the sin in which I was now drowning. Jack and I never fought, never had any harsh words, and never criticized each other for the way we were handling this difficult relationship. "I just want to maintain as much normalcy as possible," I said meekly. "Joshua is on staff there. And you have to realize how difficult it is for me to live this double life while waiting for your divorce."

I knew he understood my reasoning. At that time I didn't understand the difference between godly sorrow and worldly sorrow. I was filled with worldly sorrow. One embarrasses God's reputation, while the other only hurts your own. I was merely trying to preserve a sense of self-respect, at least in other's eyes.

I was dying a slow death. And I didn't even know it.

*****

Jack and I had previously read the book *The Five Love Languages* by Gary Chapman. We both loved it. Jack seemed to demonstrate all the qualities the book suggested. While the average person communicates in one or two of those love languages, Jack was fluent in all five love languages: words of affirmation, quality time, gifts, acts of service, and physical touch. He was almost too good to be true.

His "words of affirmation" were exactly what I needed in my lonely life. He was intentional about building me up and encouraging me to be the best I could be. He was constantly telling me how special, beautiful, and smart I was.

His commitment to our quality time together was infectious and was further proof of his undying love. If we weren't together, he was calling, texting, or e-mailing me both day and night. His connective spirit was addicting.

I can't recall a single time Jack showed up without a present, even if his "gifts" were just shells he had picked up at the beach that he thought I would love. He was also always accompanied by flowers, not to mention his occasional extravagant purchases he was constantly bestowing on me, even though I didn't really need them.

He continually dreamed up "acts of service" to help me accomplish tasks and projects around the house. Being a single woman, these tasks were certainly helpful and appreciated.

The "physical touch" he gently and passionately bestowed upon me was overwhelming. I could not get enough of Jack. My heart was open to him and even grasping for more while at the same time anguishing over the person I had become.[4] Jack had pierced my heart and had taken root deep inside my soul. At times my head tried to

---

[4] In *When Godly People Do Ungodly Things*, Beth Moore says, "Satan cannot get in from the outside without an invitation from the inside" (2004).

reason with me, but my sincere emotions overpowered any logic I once knew as truth.

As he had promised, Jack did not return to Thailand, although I knew he was still keeping in touch with Chen. Jack had previously told me he had to let Chen down slowly and couldn't just abruptly stop talking to her. He said he knew I would understand as I was such a kind and gentle person and wouldn't want to devastate someone like Chen. He also said he didn't want to disgrace Chen or her family, so he needed time for her to get used to the idea that he wouldn't be returning. After all he had already purchased her a house, met her whole family, and they were all expecting him to return to Thailand permanently.

By this point I was so insensitive to absolute right and wrong that I could no longer see truth that would be obvious to others. What woman in her right senses permits the love of her life to still communicate with the last woman he had admitted to loving (even though he claimed it was out of *sympathy* not real love)? All this while he is still married to someone else (even though he claimed it was out of *responsibility* not real love). Though still intelligent, I was not reasonable. Though seeing, I was nevertheless blind and oh so stupid! But you could have never convinced me of it.

How could all this have happened to me? I had heard the term "blinded by sin," but I never thought it was for real. I didn't realize it could prevent me from actually seeing reality. I didn't know it could affect my thought process. I didn't realize that with each choice I made to foray deeper into the Grey Zone, the scales of sin became thicker over my spiritual eyes. The thicker the scales, the deeper the sin became. I was now living in my own world, my own reality where right was wrong and wrong was right, where good was bad and bad was good.[5]

Jack's powerful displays of love and affection had totally knocked me off my feet and robbed me of my ability to discern reality.

Others might have spoken truth and wisdom into my life had I allowed someone to get that close. But I was too intoxicated with my

---

[5]   See Isaiah 5:20

own self-fulfillment and newfound "love." By definition, being blind means you are unable to see, at least on your own. Like a physically blind person cannot see color, a spiritually blind person cannot see truth. I didn't want to hear about how great "living in the truth" could be. I had grown accustomed to the dark and was content to remain there. The darkness was my new reality. Even when I heard of a man who was caught in "infidelity," my dulled senses prevented me from recognizing my own sinful lifestyle.

Unfortunately, many Christians are either too afraid or too unaware to confront friends who are caught up in a sinful lifestyle. They're too worried about hurting their feelings or losing the friend- ship. And so they sit, wait, and watch in silence, hoping and praying the sin will simply go away or that things may somehow turn out well in the end for their friend.[6]

---

[6] Beth Moore addresses in her book *When Godly People Do Ungodly Things:* "Believers can be seduced by power, by money, by position, by false doctrine, or by any number of flesh-fueling pumps…How is this best accomplished? He tries to corrupt thoughts to manipulate feelings. Satan knows that the nature of humankind is to act out of how we feel rather than what we know. One of our most important defenses against satanic influence will be learning how to behave out of what we know is *truth* rather than what we feel. Satan's desire is to modify human behavior to accomplish his unholy purposes." (Moore, 22)

Hitting the Beach

Among Jack's "toys" was a Harley-Davidson motorcycle, and he loved taking me out on rides around our hometown. Riding his Harley made Jack feel younger. He bought the bike at the same time he and I began our relationship. He loved driving along S. Ocean Boulevard and sightseeing the large waterfront homes. We cruised along Flagler, checking out the yachts. We would drive through City-Place or go down Clematis, going out for lunch at many of the wonderful restaurants there. These new adventures secretly drove me crazy because I didn't like motorcycles. Everyone could easily recognize the people on the motorcycle. This never bothered Jack. He was too busy enjoying the adventure. He told me I was being paranoid and that no one could know who we were with helmets on our heads. Though I still had my doubts, I went along with Jack's quirky desires.

Jack had long since retired from the oil business he was operating in Texas, but he now owned J. Hardie Florida Realty, which had six offices scattered from Miami to Jupiter. He was the quintessential entrepreneur, and well-known for his business exploits. Everyone recognized Jack Hardie, and yet here he was, always with a woman who was not his wife. However, he didn't think much about it, and it never seemed to bother him. On the contrary, he almost seemed to enjoy the thrill of getting caught.

One day, Jack called. "Amber, why don't you meet me at the beach tomorrow morning so we can walk along the shore together and watch the sunrise?" He knew how much I loved watching the sunrise and sunset. Jack and I both loved the beach, so we often met down at a local beach in our neighborhood, spending time walking along the shoreline. That made me nervous as well. I was always looking around to make sure we didn't see anyone we knew.

"Jack, I don't think that is too wise as we will really be out in the open with nowhere to hide."

"Why would we need to hide?" He seemed confused.

"What if we see someone we know?"

"No big deal." Jack shrugged his shoulders. "We could just say we happen to both be walking at the beach when we met. We both are allowed to go to the beach, aren't we?" Jack always seemed to put his own unique spin on things, giving them a completely different perspective.

"I guess so." I was still uncomfortable and not convinced it was a good idea. However, I loved spending time with him, and in my desperate quest for his attention, I reasoned it would probably look innocent enough should someone see us.

We met at the beach at seven o'clock on Sunday morning. Jack walked down from his home, and I parked along S. Ocean Blvd near Royal Palm Way. There weren't too many beach walkers out at that hour, but there were just enough to make me uncomfortable. Jack was so excited to see me. His little boy smile and sparkling eyes immediately began melting my unnerving emotions.

As we walked, I intentionally left some space between us, thinking that if someone saw us together we could easily explain it away. However, Jack was constantly reaching for my hand, eventually securing it in his as we walked along the water's edge.

We decided to walk north and toward the Breakers Hotel, hoping not to run into anyone we knew. Walking by each of the beachfront houses and condos, we discussed why we would or wouldn't want to live in it. We talked about the boats that passed us by, dreaming about what type of boat we would eventually purchase. We made plans for the future as we walked hand in hand on our very own neighborhood beach.

"Amber, I know you love boats and I know you love the water, but how do you feel about traveling in a coach motor home?" He sounded like a little boy in a candy store, trying to convince me to eat some of the candy.

I hesitated, processing the change in the conversation from boats to coach motor homes. "Well, I never gave it much thought, but I guess it would be really fun to travel with you that way." In reality, I was trying to contain my excitement at the thrill of such an adventure. And yet I never wanted to get my hopes up too high, just in case I lost him.

Jack seemed pleased with that response and continued, "I think we would make a good traveling team. We would also make a good ministry team. We could find soup kitchens and ministries that need our help, and we could provide needed supplies and volunteer all over the country." He smiled at me, gripping my hand. He was so proud of his idea.

I remained silent as I contemplated the future with excitement. Simultaneously, I was battling the present with lingering guilt and shame. With such opposite emotions flowing though the same heart, my soul was churning.

As we continued walking down the beach, every time we passed someone, I looked to see if I knew them or if it seemed like they knew Jack. Because the church I attended was large, many people there knew me as "Joshua's mom," even though I might not know them. But again, Jack didn't seem to care.

Jack loved scanning the shore and picking up the most beautiful shells. Each time he handed me a shell, he smiled. "I just can't wait till we are officially together so we could do this every day."

I smiled back, sincerely hoping and praying my secret life wouldn't have to be secret for too much longer.

Jack's quest for my time and attention made me believe in his undying love and unwavering commitment. During our beach walk, he assured me he just needed a little time to work out some business matters regarding his marriage and divorce, which he swore was imminent. He continually joked that if we did get caught, it would only make it easier for him to expedite divorcing Sarah, since she would be so mad that she would be the one to walk away.

Jack promised me he would never return to Thailand, but he never made that same promise regarding Guatemala. He said he had promised Juanita (whom he called J) that he would go back just one more time in February to help out with the ministry. So, as February approached, he assured me of his love and departed for the orphanage in Guatemala. It seemed to me the right thing for him to do, although I hated that he had a nickname for her too. Jack ventured off with Juanita for ten days in the mountains, getting supplies to the orphanage, and upon his return, our love appeared to be stronger than ever.

A month later Juanita came to the states to be the guest speaker at another fundraiser event for the Guatemalan orphanage held in West Palm Beach. Jack invited her to stay at his house with him and Sarah for a few days. During that time, Jack encouraged Juanita and Sarah to spend "girl time" together and go out for lunch.

It was odd that Jack wanted Juanita to spend time with Sarah as he had encouraged me to do the same. What he did not anticipate was that Sarah would confide in Juanita about the suspicions she had concerning me and Jack. Sarah told Juanita she suspected Jack and I were inappropriately involved, though not in a sexual way, since Jack had convinced Sarah he was impotent. Sarah also told Juanita about the expensive Christmas gift he had given to me.

When Juanita left to return to Guatemala, she sent Jack an e-mail, which she copied to Sarah, Colby, and other church ministry leaders saying that she was breaking off their ministry involvement together. She said she could no longer work with Jack and that he should seek help and work on his marriage.

In the e-mail, she included what Sarah told her—that Jack and I were "involved" together. She also added that she believed he carried major issues from his childhood. Jack had confided in Juanita about his dysfunctional childhood while together in the mountains of

Guatemala. (Later, Juanita and I would realize we were not the "only ones" Jack told about his supposed troubled childhood.) Juanita also mentioned in the e-mail that it was inappropriate to give "Amber" an expensive necklace for Christmas. That e-mail triggered a critical moment, threatening the secrecy of our private affair.

And Jack was understandably furious as the e-mail circulated and exposed us. Now, thanks to Juanita and Sarah, all of their ministry leaders now knew some of the secrets he and I were trying to hide. Jack agreed that his ministry relationship with Juanita was over. Jack convinced me that Juanita was unstable. He said she was not only crazy for venturing out in the mountains alone but also quite irrational for such an outrageous e-mail. He forwarded the e-mail to me (in an effort to prove his innocence) and promised he would never travel with Juanita again. After carefully reading and dissecting the e-mail together, he convinced me that Juanita was indeed crazy. Jack had a way of spinning truth into his favor.

For his part, Colby was quite upset with the information revealed in this e-mail. So Jack went into damage-control mode in an attempt to do some serious cover-up. He successfully convinced Colby, Sarah, and the ministry leaders that Juanita was just a crazy Latin American woman. He described her as an overly emotional lady who was skilled at exaggerating the facts. Jack was also mad at Sarah for disclosing such supposed personal information, persuading her to apologize to everyone for creating this unnecessary turmoil. Jack convinced everyone that he and I were two good people and that Juanita had taken Sarah's "concerns" and had blown them out of proportion. After Jack finished with his convincing story, everyone believed him.

*****

Turning to me, Jack was concerned that all this lying and covering up would damage my earned trust in him. He continually told me he eventually wanted everything out in the open between us. That's when he sat me down for a deep, straightforward conversation.

"Amber, I want you to know I realize it will be hard for you to completely trust me once we're married since you know so much about me. I know you are aware of all the lies and deceitfulness involved in an effort to hold our relationship together. I want to do everything I can so that you will develop trust in me. I am so tired of living a double life and always lying. I just want to come clean. I have told you everything so we will have no secrets between us." His voice was serious, stern, and filled with great distress.

"I trust you, Jack." I said sincerely and lovingly. "You are my best friend. And I know you have shared all kinds of buried secrets with me." I didn't like hearing Jack lie, but I also realized I too was living a lie. Though I knew Jack had lied to others, I never believed he would lie to me. "I am honored that we have such an open line of communication and a love that will survive all obstacles."

Jack said he was so worried I would not trust him explicitly as I knew he had cheated on his wife. I thought he was being overly cautious as I believed everything he was telling me. I trusted him completely.

He continued speaking in a serious tone. "Amber, after we get married, I was thinking that we should have one cell phone. This way you will be able to answer it at any time, hopefully gaining your undivided trust in me."

Though I was impressed by his excessive thoughtfulness and I appreciated his pledge to prove his faithfulness, I knew such a proposition could not practically work.

"You're being silly, Jack. What happens when we are not together? Like when you or I go to the store. Then who gets the cell phone? How would we be able to call each other if we needed something?"

"Okay, you're right. We will have two cell phones, but then we could switch off cell phones when we are with each other. This way you will know I have nothing to hide from you," Jack said.

"Jack, I trust you. That's what love is. I love you."

"We can have two cell phones, but we only need one e-mail." He looked at me. "This way you will always be able to monitor my e-mails and keep me accountable."

I didn't think that was necessary as I believed in his devotion to me. I knew how much I loved him, and I was thoroughly convinced he was sincere in his words and actions to me.

I began suspecting that the ghosts from Jack's childhood that had plagued him in the past were creeping up on his present life to torment his soul. I believed he wanted to break free from a sinful past and begin a brand-new life of love and accountability with me.

Amber "Hardie"

That spring was the very best, and worst, of my life. Jack and I were together whenever we could steal away the time. In addition, we sent an untold amount of e-mails and texts and spent endless hours talking on the phone. By anyone's estimation, we were crazy in love. For me it was like setting foot in an uncharted land. Everything was fresh, invigorating, and wonderful. Jack was attentive to my every need, and I just wanted to make him happy. We never fought, argued, disagreed, or had harsh words with one another. Quite the contrary, our countless conversations were filled with words of admiration, contentment, fulfillment, and expressions of love.

Jack regularly came over to my home, where we would sit on the couch and talk for hours about our future. We stared into each other's eyes, making promises of the life together that would surely come. We watched movies together, and Jack loved films that made him reminisce about the past or dream of the future. One of his favorites was *Shadowlands*, the life story of C. S. Lewis. In the movie, Anthony Hopkins (who plays C. S. Lewis) discovers his true love late in life (Joy Gresham) and marries her (played by Debra Winger). At first they married to keep her in the country, and Lewis continually claimed he was only "technically married." But eventually, they fell desperately in love and then Joy Gresham got ill and passed away. Jack's favorite line in the movie was, "A heart awakened to great love is also open to great pain." He often repeated scenes and lines from this movie and told me many times how much he appreciated "a true love story."

One day while Jack and I were cleaning up after lunch, he sat down at the counter and just stared at me while I maneuvered around the kitchen.

"Jack," I said, opening the refrigerator door, "stop staring at me."

His eyes were glazed over in love, fixed on me.

"You are too good for me, Amber. What are you doing with a guy like me?"

His now serious tone stopped me in me tracks. Here was Jack Hardie telling me I was too good for *him*? Right! Under the deluding influence of my desires and affections, I had the opposite perspective. He was suave and sophisticated while I was just...*regular*. Jack Hardie. Respected. Charismatic. Prominent businessman. A sought-after speaker. Educated Bible study teacher. Generous entrepreneur and international pioneer missionary.

The truth was that I felt like a nobody compared to him. I had not helped nearly as many people as Jack had helped over the years. *How could I ever really be good enough for him?*

I shut the refrigerator door and made my way around the counter, standing in front of him as he sat on the bar stool. I held his face in my hands, looking into his bright blue eyes.

"Jack, I'm not too good for you. Maybe you are too good for me," I said softly. "Or perhaps, we are just good enough for one another. How does one measure value when it comes to love?"

We sat quiet for a few seconds as we both processed our thoughts. Then we embraced, holding tightly to one another. I was certain we were both thinking about what the future would bring for the two of us.

Then suddenly Jack pulled away from me, becoming solemn. He sat up straight and caressed my shoulders with one hand while running his fingers through my curly black hair with the other. He carefully examined my face.

"I cannot wait to marry you and make you my wife, Amber Hardie."

His words were like a knife stabbing my heart as I intensely disliked it when he referred to me that way. I didn't mind his affectionate nicknames, but "Amber *Hardie*" sent my stomach into convulsions. Secretly, of course, I couldn't wait to take on his last name. But I knew that attaching his last name to me right now was just plain wrong.

Oh, the irony of me judging something as "wrong" during a time when there were so many gaps in my moral boundaries that they hardly existed at all. I was having an affair with a married man, and yet something so simple as verbally attaching my first name with Jack's last name deeply disturbed me.

"Someday they should make a movie of our love story. A love so strong, that against all odds, it would overcome and survive." Jack pushed the curls off my face. "It will be the story of two caring people from different generations, two souls destined to be together." He smiled and hugged me tightly.

I loved his warm embrace and, despite my discomfort at his previous statement, I wished I could capture this moment and live in it forever.

I pulled away enough to look into his smiling face, smiling back. "Maybe someday I will write a book about the undying, steadfast love of two people and the amazing moments they shared together."

He reached for my hair, and after twirling it gently in his fingers, he pushed it behind my shoulders. Tenderly touching my face, he caressed my shoulders, agreeing, "You do that, Amby. I can't wait to read it."

Hit-and-Run

In June of that same year, we were all shocked when Jack was diagnosed with colon cancer. Like everything else in his life, Jack handled it with dignity and resolve. We educated ourselves concerning the illness and discussed various treatment options. Jack scheduled a phone conversation with his doctor and wanted me to listen in so I could help advise him regarding treatment. He was supposed to arrive at my home early so we would have some time together before the phone call, but he was late, and that was very unlike him. Being an ex-military man, Jack was always a punctual person. His tardiness worried me, and I wondered where he might be.

What I did not know at the time was that while Jack was on his way to my home, he unknowingly passed Sarah heading in the opposite direction. She had gone out that morning with some friends. When her plans had been cancelled at the last minute, she was returning home unexpectedly.

Jack didn't see his wife make an abrupt U-turn and begin following him toward my house. She saw him come to stop at an intersection on my street, less than a block from my home. Sarah pulled up behind him. She opened her car door, got out, and proceeded to walk toward Jack's car. Jack recognized Sarah and her car in the rear-view mirror and got out to meet her on the street. Sarah was fuming mad. She did an about-face and got back in her car. She floored the gas pedal and ran her Jaguar right into the back of Jack's BMW.

At this point Jack was returning to his car and got caught half in and half out. As the door violently slammed on him, he held on for his life. The impact of her car rear-ending his caused Jack to be dragged over the curb as she pushed the car up on the sidewalk, running over the stop sign, and crashing into a building. Jack fell helplessly to the pavement and lay there bleeding as Sarah then backed up and recklessly sped off down the road.

A passerby witnessed the incident and called 911. The police and ambulance soon arrived, but Jack refused treatment. He never admitted to knowing who had done this, choosing instead to make everyone believe it was simply a case of hit-and-run. His badly damaged car needed to be towed, and the Good Samaritan who had witnessed the accident drove Jack to my house.

I couldn't imagine what was keeping Jack from arriving, but I soon found out. Stumbling through the front door in shock, with blood oozing through his pants leg and dripping down from his elbow, Jack was mumbling.

"She tried to kill me, Amber. She tried to kill me!"

Jack was convinced Sarah had finally snapped and officially gone crazy. Looking at the badly bruised and bleeding man sitting in front of me, I had no reason not to believe him. I felt terrible. Deep in my heart I knew I may have reacted the same way had I been in Sarah's spot. Indeed, hell hath no fury like a woman scorned.

Jack immediately called his son to go calm Sarah down and make sure she wouldn't do anything else crazy. He also called Colby and his wife, Ella, asking if they would go be with Sarah as he believed she might actually become suicidal.

This horrible incident let our secret out of the bag. Everyone now knew there was something going on between me and Jack. We had been able to quell rumors concerning the expensive Christmas present and spin Juanita's e-mail to our advantage. But Jack coming to my house in the middle of the morning was something that would be much more difficult to explain. Secret sin on earth is open scandal in heaven.

In spite of this looming reality, Jack didn't want to go home. He preferred staying indefinitely at my house, something I didn't think was a good idea, and I told him as much. Although blinded to many glaring sins in my life, I still didn't want to be known as the "other woman." I suggested it would be best for Jack to leave and check into a hotel. We called and booked a room at a local extended suite hotel. Jack would be able to stay there for an indefinite period of time, at least until the divorce was final. And surely with this unfortunate incident, we concluded, would expedite that process.

When Jack knew Sarah would not be at home, he snuck over to collect some of his clothes, belongings, and pictures. Then he moved into the hotel suite. Jack felt extremely lonely, hurt, and overwhelmed at the thought of his wife trying to "kill" him, especially in light of his recent diagnosis of colon cancer. He needed time to contemplate his next move, and during the following days, we processed it together.

Earlier in our relationship I had sworn to myself I would never go to a hotel with Jack. In my mind, meeting in a hotel room was the epitome of a sinful relationship. And yet here I was in his room. The hotel room of a married man. A man with whom I, a professing Christian, was having an illicit relationship. Later, I would look back and wonder how I managed to compromise the very values I had preached to my own children. How could I have done the very things I had sought to protect my friends and loved ones from doing?[7]

Of course, at the time I reasoned that it really didn't make a difference if I was intimate with Jack in my home or in a hotel room. Location didn't make one right and the other wrong. After all Jack kept reminding me that he was only "technically married" anyway. This was now his favorite line.

---

[7]   Beth Moore says, "If we could only understand that the devil does not work haphazardly but carefully, methodically, weaving and spinning, and watching for just the right time." Ibid.

The season that followed was bittersweet for me. Since Jack was now out of his house, we were able to spend wonderful days together, days which, for the first time, turned into evenings. Neither of us had to "rush" home. We spent hours dreaming of what would be and how we were going to work it out.

*****

Jack had taken some pictures and photo albums from his house, and one evening we sat and looked at them one by one. He had pictures from his childhood, of him when he was in the Marines, and various photos depicting his life throughout the years. He even had extra pictures made for me, just so I would have them. I stared at those pictures, thinking how handsome and young he looked in his Marine uniform. It was easy to see how Sarah fell in love with him. I felt honored to have pictures of Jack for my own keeping and thrilled to learn more about his life through them.

My descending spiral of sin was now reaching new depths. What began as seemingly insignificant decisions were now altering the entire course of my life, redefining my heart, mind, and soul. And since no man, and woman, is an island, it would affect the lives of those I loved the most. This spiritual battle was about to get bloody.

The Bible says, "Flee from sexual immorality. All other sins a person commits are outside the body, but whoever sins sexually, sins against their own body" (1 Cor. 6:18). I was sinning against God, my family, Jack, Sarah, and even myself. But it didn't matter.

At this point we had both resigned from the ministries we had previously represented. No more funding the orphanage in Thailand or the one in Guatemala. I had turned over all of my responsibilities for the fund-raising, the sponsorship program, and maintaining of records to others. I eventually heard these people were not doing a good job keeping up with sponsors and donations, so both orphanages were suffering from lack of funding.

Jack no longer visited the orphanages to check up on the children and the staff. I felt terrible for the kids, like I was abandoning them. But I believed this to be temporary situation. As soon as Jack and I were officially married, we would be able to help each orphanage again…as a couple.

Jack had also resigned from the church and refused to speak to pastors when they attempted to reach out to him. I, on the other hand, had not resigned from the church since my son was the worship leader there. So, in my infinite wisdom, I thought it best at the time to simply deny everything and play dumb.

Of course, I had some great coaching from Jack, who helped me carefully organize my story, thoughts, and every move. However, when I received a call from the church office to come meet with one of the pastors, Jack strongly urged me not to go, being quite adamant about it. But I assured him I could play it cool and breeze my way through the conversation.

After all, I really believed the lie I was living. And perception, even self-perception, is *reality*. I believed Jack and I belonged together and that he was going to divorce Sarah regardless of me. I also believed I had nobly saved Jack from the dreadful mistake of leaving the country. However, I would never tell anyone that, as I needed to protect Jack regarding his infidelity, both foreign and domestic.[8]

*****

Unbeknownst to me, Jack was inadvertently teaching me the art of *obfuscation*. I had never even heard the word before. However, Jack loved the word *obfuscate*. He taught me that to obfuscate means to make something obscure or unclear. He should know, as Jack was a master at not telling the whole truth. He taught me how to muddy up a conversation and make it confusing. He explained that if you just answer someone's question with a short yes or no, they tend to draw their own conclusions, never really expecting the lie that you

---

[8] In *Invitations from God*, Adele Ahlberg Calhoun, tells us: "Sin separates and isolates. Brennan Manning writes, 'Sin is the starting point of all social estrangement. Every sin…leaves its mark on the psychic structure of the human soul. Every unrepentant sin has a sinisterly obscuring effect on true openness.' Sin is how we destroy ourselves. It is its own penalty. It diminishes our ability to receive and closes us down to truth, to God, and to others." (115)

could be hiding. *Obfuscate* became my new word…and the background music to my life.

Even so, I still believed that Jack and I were two good people trying to do good, serve God, and do God's will. I believed Jack had been unhappily married for forty plus years and thus deserved more. To me, Sarah was somewhat psychotic and did not understand Jack, making him so miserable he was willing to move to Thailand to get away from her and start over in life. I saw Jack as a person of character and integrity and a man who genuinely loved the Lord. He was going to be the spiritual leader of our little family. We were gifts to each other and destined to be together. I knew Jack loved me and that the best was yet to come. His temporary situation of being only "technically" married would soon come to an end.

As I considered Sarah's mental state and her attempt to do him harm, it all started making sense to me.

Why else would he give me a gun for my protection? Why would he give me a mini-high beam flashlight for the side of my bed in case of an emergency? Why would he put extra locks on my doors? Why would he install a house alarm? It has to be because Sarah is a genuine risk to harm me or Jack. And why would Jack give me pictures of himself when he was a child and pictures of him in the Marines if he did not love me and want me to know everything about him?

For me, these seemed like authentic acts of love. Jack always defined love this way: "Love is what you do, not what you say. Anyone could say 'I love you,' but true love is what you *do*." Because I had never experienced this type of caring, protection, and love, I was only too pleased to embrace it with all my heart.

Had you put me under a lie detector test, I would have told you Jack and I were truly in love. That's how sincerely I believed our love was real and that it was justified. Sadly, our church friends did not understand the depth of what was going on in our lives. They were the blind ones, not us. Not me. I believed God actually wanted us to be married so we could travel together and serve foreign ministries.

Knowing and believing all these things, going to the church office would be a cakewalk. At least that's what I thought. However,

I didn't realize what would happen when I got there. When I arrived, not only was my pastor there, but Colby was as well.

They began grilling me about what was going on with me and Jack and why he was headed to my house in the first place on the day of the accident. They questioned me about why I had accepted an expensive Christmas present from a married man and why we were spending so much time together. They probed more about the car accident, and they wanted to know the real reasons we had both resigned from the ministries we were serving.

During the course of my interrogation, it became clear to me that these two men (who were also Jack's former close friends) were blaming *me* for this relationship. I felt cornered. Trapped. Degraded. Their line of questioning and the looks on their faces told me they were profoundly disappointed that I was ruining this man's life.

They insisted I end the inappropriate relationship immediately. I defended myself, insisting they were dead wrong about us and that they just didn't understand. There was no way I was going to sell Jack out and tell them of his plan to leave the country or how he never loved his wife. I basically pled the Fifth, remaining quiet and letting them believe I really was the one to blame.

I had been a good pupil. And now I was testing my skills at obfuscation.

*****

Much later I would read the words of Beth Moore, who adequately describes this spiritual state:

> Deception is an absolute in every stronghold, but the nature of seductive deception is that the lies are often well masked for a while. We are undoubtedly caught in a stronghold of deception when we realize we're starting to "have to lie" to explain our behavior. We reason with ourselves

that others just wouldn't understand, but the real reason is that the deceived soon deceive.[9]

I believed I could easily hide what was so blatantly obvious to others. I did tell the men I would not turn my back on Jack in his time of need, as he was my good friend and I intended to keep it that way.

Leaving the church office that June day, I was a complete emotional mess. Having kept my composure together while there, as soon as I left, I began quivering and crying over the lie I was living, a lie that was tearing the fabric of my life apart. When I related to Jack what had transpired, he was furious with the two men for cornering me that way.

"It was an ambush!" he declared. He was also upset I had gone against his will.

But I wasn't that worried as I thought I could straighten everything out while maintaining my good reputation.

But who was I fooling? Keep "my good reputation"? I was involved with a married man. My reputation was coming unglued. How does something like this happen? How does an intelligent woman like me become so desperately stupid? How was I possibly going to "straighten everything out"? My poor choices had dictated a new life course and one for which I was not prepared to travel. I was desperately trying to make my sin "right" buy sinning even more! What I could not see was that my lifestyle had ruined my good reputation. My sin's powerful seduction had a grip on my life, and I could not break free.[10]

The damage was done, and I could only hope the two men would believe my side of the story. Jack's strategy, however, was to remain absent, unavailable, and silent.

---

[9] Moore, 43–44.

[10] Beth Moore writes, "Seduction is a form of oppression, of course, but it's a very sly scheme intended to catch us off guard, pitched with mind-boggling velocity from a direction we were not expecting. Seduction means the demonic trickery of a professional liar...Seduction is Satan at his *best*." Ibid, 187.

Motor Home

Jack convinced me that our future involved traveling around the world together. He wanted to take me to Italy, the country of love. He promised to take me to Thailand and Guatemala, to once again shower love on the children in the orphanages we had helped. He envisioned us traveling the US, seeing all the sights and experiencing the beauty God had created. We planned to go hot air ballooning in the Napa Valley, fly over the Grand Canyon, to boat under Niagara Falls, and to explore the nation's beaches.

Since we both loved long walks on the beach and romantic sunsets, we talked again about owning a condo on the Florida coastline. We had decided that in the near future we would buy a coach motor home so we could disappear on long trips together. And in light of the criticism and disapproval we were receiving from church friends, this seemed like a great idea. So Jack persuaded me to go shopping with him for motor homes. We looked at forty-five-foot coach motor homes, touring one after another, trying to pick just the right one to live on for an indefinite amount of time.

I couldn't help but think that John, the motor home salesman, was looking at us suspiciously. I felt like the "other woman" while exploring the motor homes. Jack, on the other hand, was quite giddy at the possibility of leaving town. As we stepped inside the huge vehicles, Jack beamed with excitement.

"Oh, Amber, this one is beautiful," he announced. "It has stainless steel appliances, a king-size bed, and a split bathroom in the middle. What do you think?"

John, the salesman, turned cautiously to watch for my approval and to assess the potential sale. I felt uneasy. "I love it. It is huge and the interior is beautiful." I was still not convinced leaving town this way was a good idea.

Meanwhile, Jack was like a kid in a candy store, so thrilled to take me shopping for a motor home. Keeping the momentum rolling, he said to the salesman, "John, I want Amby here to be happy. Let's look at some others so she can compare them and get the one she wants."

We went in and out of multiple motor homes that day. Along the way, John was fishing for information about our relationship and our use for the motor home.

"So, what business are you in, Mr. Hardie?"

Jack was only too happy to brag about his successful career. "I am the retired CEO and president of a major oil company in Texas. And Amber and I are about to embark on a major trip together." Jack refrained from saying anything about the real estate firm, and I wondered if John might have recognized him. After all everyone knew Jack Hardie.

A slight tension filled the air.

"Do you have any others to show us?" I said.

"Sure," John replied. "They are all in a row. Let's keep looking. After all," he said, turning toward Jack, "we want Amber to be happy, right?" John smiled at Jack, willing to do whatever it took to make a quick sale.

The next one we looked at not only had stainless steel appliances and a king-size bed, but also two bathrooms, one in the middle and one in the back. "Oh, now this one is great, Jack," I blurted, while holding on to his arm. "The master bath in the back is roomy and offers privacy and the one in the middle is for guests." I turned to John. "Jack's dream includes having friends and family stay with us on occasion."

Jack laughed. "I only want to make you happy. You have a vote in this too…okay then. Two bathrooms it is!"

We laughed at our apparent compromise as my heart began to soften to the idea of traveling.

John just looked at us in bewilderment as if to say, "So are we getting this one today?"

Jack asked John for some privacy in the motor home, and John gladly went outside hoping this would be the quickest sale of the year. Jack asked me to sit next to him on the comfy couch, holding both my hands and looking into my eyes.

"Amber, let's buy a motor home today and start traveling. We could purchase this one. The one you like with the two bathrooms. It has great lighting and a beautiful living area. The bedroom is large, and it has plenty of special storage areas. The hydraulics are great and the living room and bedroom will expand to give us more room. The living room even extends to a deck with a canopy. It's the best!"

While John was outside, hoping to sell to Jack, he was inside putting the hard sell on me.

"Let's just leave town right now. Please, let's just go ahead and start our new life together. We have been together for almost a year now, and we need to go ahead and jump in and get on with it."

My heart was torn as I listened and thought of traveling the country in this beautiful coach motor home with the man of my dreams. And yet, at that moment, reality came crashing over me like a bucket of ice water.

"Jack, I can't just run out of town with you while you are still married." In truth, part of me desperately wanted to leave with him, but what little reason I had left longed to stay for my "good reputation." "If I leave with you now, everyone will know we have been involved all this time. I just can't do that." I was deeply confused over right and wrong but still trying to figure out how I could somehow make it all right. Leaving with Jack seemed so wonderful. It would fulfill a lifetime of dreams. It would also make public our very private relationship and forever stain my reputation.

Jack became more persistent. "Amber, don't you think people will figure it all out anyway when we leave town together after the divorce?"

I hesitated. "Well, yes. I guess people will figure out we fell in love before the divorce. However, maybe they will think we waited to be together until after the divorce was final." Even I was having trouble believing that one.

Jack sat up straight. He began caressing my arms and shoulders as his bright blue eyes locked on mine. His face was serious. "I doubt that very much, Amber."

We sat quietly trying to work through various "solutions," none of which were very good or right. Jack stroked my hair.

"Amber, people aren't stupid. They will figure it all out. So let's just go. Let's start our dream now."

At this point, I was upset. I was so torn as I always wanted to make Jack happy. But in the end I was unable to give in to his passionate pleas. It made me feel disoriented. I broke away from the trance he had me in, standing to my feet. I began pacing the living room/kitchen area in circles.

"Oh, Jack," I cried. "You know I want to go. You know how much I love you. But I just can't leave. Not *this* way. I have to do it right."

Jack stood up and held me tight to calm down my fears. Pressing my head into his chest, he gently rubbed my back. Jack knew just how to diffuse a tense situation, especially with me.

We exited the motor home, holding hands, to find John quietly standing there with a smile on his face and dollars signs in his eyes. Jack approached him with a confident handshake.

"John, Amber and I are going to think about this for a day or two. However, I *will* be back." Jack smiled at John, giving his hand a final squeeze.

I am sure John felt like this was the big fish that somehow got away. But I was glad. And the two of us walked away, hand in hand.

23

Taking a Break

Jack and I had finally become a "real couple." We sat by the hotel pool during the day, watched movies in the evening, and slept together at night. Every day was one day closer to our dream becoming a reality. Jack kept prodding me, saying our dream would be complete if only I would just leave town with him in the motor home.

Then one afternoon Jack's phone rang. It was Sarah, and she was sobbing uncontrollably. She started explaining how sorry she was for "running Jack off the road. I thought, *What an oversimplification, seeing as how she practically tried to kill him, almost running over him!* But no matter what version of the story one tells, Sarah had reached an emotional breaking point. I was right there with Jack when she called and could hear her voice on the other end of the phone. Sarah pleaded for Jack to come home, begging for his forgiveness.

However, in the same conversation, Sarah also revealed how upset she was over an e-mail she had mistakenly received. Evidently, as Jack was erasing e-mails, he inadvertently sent one to Sarah that was meant for me. It was an email expressing just how much he loved me. Jack became immediately suspicious that Sarah had gained access to his private e-mails. So, mixed in with her emotional apology, was her displeasure at Jack's relationship with me.

"I can't understand how you could jeopardize your integrity and good name by entering into such an inappropriate relationship with *her*," Sarah cried.

Her apologetic, yet angry, voice was so loud, I had no trouble hearing every word.

Jack remained his usual calm self, patiently listening. When she was finished, Jack tried explaining to her that it was over between them and that he did not love her anymore.

Even so, she persisted. Seeing that her emotional rant did nothing to win him back, she switched into more of a steady and quiet voice. "Jack, I am so sorry for trying to run you over. Please come home to me."

"I *don't* love you, Sarah. Please, leave it alone. It's over," Jack said firmly.

Hearing Jack's definitive words, my heart actually broke for Sarah and I felt a degree of sympathy for her. Jack didn't love her, but I knew she still loved him. But Jack had never been in love with Sarah, which was why he was never faithful to her. In a twisted sort of way, I believed I was doing her a favor by freeing her of a man who never loved her. Jack had convinced me that, like us, Sarah also deserved to find love. He said it wasn't fair for Sarah to live in a loveless marriage, especially since she believed he was impotent. So my compassion for Sarah moved me to believe she deserved more. She deserved a man who really loved her, and Jack was neither in love with her nor available for her. She had her chance with him, and he was mine now.

"Sarah, it's over. I do not love you," he said again. And with that he hung up the phone, clearly upset and resolutely determined to leave her.

After that dramatic phone call, Jack had me help him change the password on his e-mail account. We also erased the "extra" Thailand ministry e-mail account he had set up for "business." I was only too happy to get rid of it.

Having previously vowed he would no longer talk to Nyri or Chen, he now told me that enough time had passed for him to contact Chen and convince her that he was not coming back to marry her and start another orphanage. He accomplished this by confusing and darkening the story, only telling her part of the truth. Jack revealed to Chen that his health was not well and that he would need the kind of medical treatment available in the West that wasn't accessible in Asia. That part was true and it made sense, both to me and to Chen. And because Chen wanted him to get the best medical treatment possible, she accepted his explanation.

The last time Jack was in Thailand was the previous August. It was now June. I knew he was still occasionally communicating with Chen, so I was relieved to know it was now officially over. Jack said he had to let her down slowly and to avoid disgracing her, her family, or her culture. I was only too glad to erase the e-mail account so Jack wouldn't contact Chen anymore. And after changing his e-mail passwords, I was relieved knowing Sarah would no longer have access to his e-mails. Jack also asked me to go into his cell phone account and change the online passwords. Then we changed his mailing address to a PO Box so Sarah could not gain access to his phone bills and other accounts.

I did all these things willingly, having become so blinded to right and wrong that blatantly sinful situations become natural to me. My conscience was seared, cauterized, and numb to God's Spirit and His truth. Normally, I would have known I was in a deadly situation. Huge red flags waving right under my nose. Everywhere I turned, neon signs were flashing, "*Run!*" "*Seek Help!*" "*Think!*" But I ignored them all in light of the satisfaction and fulfillment I was experiencing.

Jack was the love of my life. To me, he was still a man with character and integrity and he loved me as passionately as I loved him. Though we were sailing through uncharted waters, someday this would all make sense. Someday it will all be okay. At least that's what I kept telling myself.

Following that phone call, we sat down and wrote out all the options concerning how we could expedite our being together. None of them were feasible at the time. Jack continued lobbying for us to run away together; however, I insisted he be divorced first before formally announcing our relationship. Jack's regular comeback response was, "Amber, people are going to figure it out anyway."

But I didn't want people to figure it out. And I certainly didn't want to be forever branded as the "other woman." So whereas Jack wanted things to happen fast, I wanted them to happen "right."

"Right?" What did that even mean anymore? "Right" to me was simply what "felt right." What I want "right." I determined "right" and "wrong" based upon expediency or how it made me feel at the time. My view of morality had moved from absolute to relative as I had continually readjusted it based on what I thought was best for me. Had I measured myself up against God's standards, I would have come up woefully short. But *I* had become my own standard. I was having an affair with a married man. God condemns it, yet I rationalized it, based somewhat on Jack's assertion that he was only "technically" married. So how could I ever be "right" in a relationship like that?

*****

After a few more days of debating what we should do, I dropped a bombshell on Jack, telling him I could no longer see him until he was officially divorced. I had reached a crossroads, and instead of continuing straight, I had to pull over and park in order to do some serious thinking. My head was spinning, and my life was out of control. No longer able to think straight, I desperately needed time away from him so I could try and get my life back on track. If Jack and I were ever to be together, it had to wait until the dust had settled from his divorce with Sarah. It simply couldn't happen while he was in the middle of it. I'm sure this sudden, uncharacteristic display of sensibility and courage didn't come from me. I was too blind, numb, and in the darkness to arrive at such a conclusion. Rather, it had to have been energized by the Holy Spirit, who had lain so dormant within me these many months. I was, by no means, out of the woods yet in my sinful stupor. But that decision, the first good one I had made in a long while, was a step forward and toward God and the Amber I once was.

Jack used my decision as an opportunity to move back home and to be in a comfortable environment in light of his upcoming cancer treatments. Understandably, he did not want to be in small hotel room all alone.

For the rest of that summer, we had a much-needed break from each other. This also allowed the rumors about us to slowly fade from the headlines. With our church friends hot on our trail, being apart was a good thing. Jack also needed to work on some things in his own life, promising to get his finances in order, sell off the real estate firm, put his house on the market, and wean his life away from Sarah.

Jack had always contended that if we were "discovered," it would expedite his divorce. But when his own wife discovered our relationship, it only led to him back home to Sarah.

My son Joshua and wife, Shanna, had been out of the country for three weeks while all this was happening. Upon their return home, I chose to sit down with Joshua and Shanna and admit to what had happened while they were away. I wanted to confess my indiscretions before any of our mutual friends spoke to them.

To be honest, I was somewhat surprised that no one had contacted them yet. Joshua, Shanna, and I sat on the couch and cried while I poured out my heart concerning my life of sin. I told them all about the affair, the hit-and-run, the meeting with Colby and the pastor, and the lies. The pain of confessing this to my own children was unbearable. I felt like an avalanche of shame had descended upon me. I had always been the spiritual leader of my home. Always been the voice of reason—the Sunday school teacher, youth leader, small group teacher, and godly mother. But through a series of decisions leading me into the grey, I had come to no longer resemble the woman I once was. And now, with these revelations, I was shattering the image they had long held of me.

At the end of our time together, I assured both Joshua and Shanna that my present relationship with Jack was over. Thankfully, they were gracious and forgiving and expressed their undying love for me. And yet the kindness they demonstrated made my pain that much more severe.

How could I have done this to them? How did all this happen? At what point did I stop abiding with Christ? How did I not recognize the increasing shades of grey and not slam on the breaks? How could I have forgotten what I had taught my children over the past twenty-five years?

This began a season where I struggled desperately to get my heart right with God. However, I couldn't help wonder if I could still be a good Christian while waiting to be with a man who was presently seeking a divorce? I sincerely thought I could. I started going to church regularly. I even met with Dorothy, our woman's ministry leader. Dorothy gave me the book *When Godly People Do Ungodly Things* by Beth Moore. I read the book, but it was more like reading a newspaper. It was information, but what I needed was *transformation*. My heart was still suffering from the effects of long-term hardening. My vision, though improved enough to take a few positive steps forward, was still blinded. My soul was not in the right place. My mind was still focused on my future with Jack. Although I thought I was seeking God and seeking help, I was doing it on my own terms and not God's. I would later learn that worship is that affection which captivates our heart and mind. And by that definition, I was worshipping Jack Hardie.

I used this time in my life to reconnect at church, read my Bible, and even meet with Dorothy for counsel. I was resolute in my stand not to be with Jack again unless he was divorced. I believed I was on the right track. And on the outside, it may have appeared that way.

We spent all of July and August apart. Still, we kept in contact through e-mails and daily phone calls. I discovered how difficult it is to tear yourself apart from the man who had been woven into the fabric of my everyday life for the last year. It was torture for us to not see each other. However, we continued pledging our undying love and patiently waited for the town chatter to die down and for Jack to proceed with the divorce.

24

Waterfront Retreat

The beginning of September marked the end of Jack's cancer treatments, and thankfully, he received a clean bill of health. With his strength returned, he left Sarah again, moving to another home he owned in Fort Lauderdale, about an hour away from Palm Beach. I saw this as a perfect retreat for us, with a pool right on the water and a boat in the back. Jack was again "officially" separated from Sarah, and once again I fell back into my old way of thinking, and we became a couple again. Since we were now an hour from our hometown, we felt free to go out in public together. We frequented all the local restaurants on Las Olas Blvd. and went shopping at the Sawgrass and Galleria Malls. We went to the movies, Fort Lauderdale beach, and local parks. We swam and played tennis, and Jack started teaching me to play golf. At night, after a nice dinner we watched endless movies together.

We also took the boat out on the water and watched the sunset. Jack taught me how to operate the boat, and I was beginning to get quite good at playing "captain." We spent hours shooting pool, and he taught me how to throw darts at a local pub.

For my part I was teaching Jack how to cook; and before long he was making the best dinners, complete with flowers, candles, and wine. He was thoroughly enjoying his newfound hobby of cooking; and that, combined with his innate gift of serving, made mealtimes something I looked forward to.

*****

One afternoon that September, I arrived at the Fort Lauderdale home just as the crab legs were coming off the stove. Opening the door, I could hear soft music playing and observed Jack in the kitchen frantically trying to get ready. He looked so cute, simultaneously balancing the timing of the crab legs, the vegetables, and the melted butter. I knew how much he loved taking me out for dinner, but he seemed to be getting a special kind of satisfaction at this new cooking adventure.

Jack placed the flowers on the corner of the table. "Amber, have a seat. I am all ready for you." He raced around the kitchen like a little boy with new toys. "I hope you're hungry." Setting the pot down, he walked over to the table where I was standing. Placing his arms around me, he looked into my eyes and paused. Giving me a tight hug and a gentle kiss, he said, "I am so glad to see you."

"I am happy to see you too," I responded, hugging him back.

We stood there in a prolonged embrace. Then Jack pulled out my chair for me. "Sit right here, my dear," placing the napkin on my lap like a proper maître d.

"What service!" I remarked, laughing.

Jack lit the candles on the table and dimmed the lights. I tried to get up to help him with the food, but he would not hear of it.

With the table now all set and the food in its rightful place, Jack sat down and took my hands in his. We sat in silence for a few moments while Jack gently caressed my hands. I admired his salt-and-pepper-colored hair reflecting the candlelight glow.

"Well then, the food is going to get cold. Let's pray," he said with a smile.

Despite the state we were in, we still both acknowledged God in our relationship. I loved to hear Jack pray. His strong voice and compassionate prayers always warmed my heart. I was just so grateful to finally have a strong spiritual leader in my life, and one who genuinely loved God. I convinced myself I had found the spiritual man of my dreams.

"Dear heavenly Father, I thank you for Amber. I pray you will bless all our children in the orphanages that we serve. I pray for their safety, and I pray that you will provide for them until the time when we are able to get back to visit and help them. I pray you will protect Amber for me until we are able to be together. Please bless this food we are about to eat and nourish it to our bodies so that we would have the strength to serve you. I pray this in your precious and holy name, our almighty God. Amen."

His prayers were music to my ears melting my heart. Jack knew I loved hearing him pray. He gave me a gentle kiss as he let go of my hands. I reached up to gently stroke his cheeks.

"I love you so much, Jack Hardie."

He simply whispered, "Ah yes, but I love you more."

We had so much fun together at the waterfront house. As a couple, we never fought, argued, or exchanged harsh words. On the contrary, we were constantly encouraging one another. Jack taught me to believe in myself, how to relax and enjoy the colors of a sunset. But perhaps the most important thing he showed me was that "Love is what you *do*, not what you *say*." I believed him, and that phrase became a repeated refrain in our relationship.

I had always loved the water, and having a boat was so gratifying. And since Jack was so skilled at event planning, he would prepare picnics of cheese and apples, shrimp and cocktail sauce, fruit and crackers, and, of course, wine to take with us on our boat excursions.

On one of those trips, we had planned to be on the water all day. We rode down the coast sightseeing the waterfront homes before Jack found a quiet place away from other boats and dropped anchor there. I spread out a blanket on the bow of the boat and we both just lay there, staring up at the sky.

Because Jack was always in high gear, getting him to relax was quite an achievement.

He was also not used to experiencing nature, so getting him to stop long enough to look at the clouds was quite an accomplishment. However, the gentle rocking of the boat created a relaxing sway. We lay there on our backs, looking at the sky.

"It looks like a rabbit. Do you see it, Jack?"

"Where? What are you talking about?" he retorted in a serious tone.

"The cloud, Jack. Look at the cloud." I held his face and pointed it in the direction of the cloud. "Can you see the two eyes and the rabbit ears?"

Jack peered up at the cloud formations in an attempt to appease me, but did not see anything.

I pressed him. "Jack, just look at the sky with imagination and find something in the clouds. I see a rabbit. What do you see?"

"Oh, I see it now!" he exclaimed, sitting straight up.

I laughed at his newfound amazement.

"There it is. The ears. The eyes. The nose. I see the rabbit," he said.

"What else can you see?" I asked as we swayed side by side in the boat.

Jack gazed upward for a while, then reported, "Over there. I see a soldier." He seemed so proud of himself, now that he was "seeing." He continued, "He has a hat and a face with a long body, and arms at his side."

"Yes. I see it," I said, laughing. "But the clouds are moving fast, and now it looks like a clown."

Jack chuckled, hugging me tight. Leaning up on one arm, he looked down into my eyes. "I cannot wait to watch the sunset with you tonight. His face then grew somber. "I never appreciated a sunset until you came into my life. I always thought watching them was a waste of time. I just never understood why people would want to waste time watching the same sun every day. But you have taught me to appreciate the beautiful colors and the unique magnificence of the sky each day. You have opened up a whole new world to me. I now appreciate the setting of the sun, the anticipation of the new day, and the exciting things it brings. I love sunsets…and now, today you've taught me to see beauty in the clouds. You are *my* Amber. I love you, Amber Hardie."

I once again cringed inside as he prematurely added his last name to mine. Even though I knew our relationship was totally inappropriate, hearing that phrase formed a knot in my stomach. I managed to keep a straight face. Jack rolled over on his back and looked up at the clouds again, smiling.

Lying there in silence, I went back to processing our sinful relationship. It's funny how a few simple words could jolt me into a moment of clarity. We were wrong for the life we were living, and for the love we were sharing. Yet, day after day, I was engrossed in our relationship without giving much thought to how sinful it was. But anytime Jack called me "Amber Hardie," I froze and was reminded of how wrong we were.

Jack somehow always knew what I was thinking. "I see a motor home in the clouds. Do you see it?" he said, breaking both the silence as well as the tension.

We both laughed as Jack started tickling me until I cried with laughter.

That evening we docked at our favorite harborside restaurant. I had become skilled at operating the boat and even bringing it in to dock. Jack snickered at my seriousness toward my newfound boating ability. But even when I came in crooked or accidently hit the dock post, he just smiled and encouraged me.

"Great job. You'll do better next time."

He *continually* encouraged me to be more than I ever thought I could be.

*****

That fall I spent more time at the Fort Lauderdale harbor home than I did at my own. Although I put up a good façade in front of Jack, inside I was a miserable mess. I was living a lie and a double life. This forced me to habitually obfuscate" I would spend a few blissful days living with Jack in Fort Lauderdale and then go home to "regroup," as I called it. I would make a family appearance, show up at church, and greet the neighbors like I had been there all along. I watered my plants, checked my mail, and paid my bills. I discovered that living two lives required a lot of effort. But to me it was worth it to finally have the life I had always dreamed about.

The Unexpected Visitor

One December morning, after returning from brunch at our favorite restaurant, Jack and I were relaxing in the poolside lanai. Our two lounge chairs were right next to each other so we could be close enough to hold hands. On either side was an end table with a glass of wine. Jack's music was softly playing on the Bose sound system. I learned to love and appreciate the music from his generation. It was a nice day, and we were grateful for the relieving cooler weather. That put us in the mood to discuss decorating the Fort Lauderdale home for the holidays. We also began discussing Christmas presents. Jack was an expert present giver. I, on the other hand, always had a hard time trying to think of a present for a man who literally has everything.

As we sat there, I suddenly realized there were two screen doors leading into the enclosed pool area, one on the left and one on the right. It occurred to me if anyone entered through one of those screen doors, they could look right into the den window, living room window, or even the bedroom window. That realization made me extremely uncomfortable, so I brought it up to him.

"So, Jack, do you realize that someone could come in the lanai and then see through the windows?"

Jack looked around in bewilderment, then laughed. "Who would want to look in our windows?"

I didn't return the laughter but became more determined to make him take the matter seriously.

"What about a private detective?" I asked.

Jack's laugh got louder, and he squeezed my hand harder. "Are you serious? You are so paranoid...relax." He smiled at me, adding his famous wink.

But I was still not convinced and certainly not relaxed. Getting up from my chaise lounge, I went over to the bedroom window, placing my face to the glass and my hands on either side of my head. "See? I can look right in between the blinds, even though they are shut. You just have to get up close enough so you could see through the tiny holes. Then you could see right into the room." I walked around along the windows, doing the same thing. The thought of someone looking into the bedroom made me sick.

Jack was still not convinced and instead was somewhat perplexed.

"And why would a private detective press his face on our glass just to look through our bedroom windows?" Jack inquired.

"Well, what if someone hired a private detective to catch us together?"

"And who would do that?" Jack nonchalantly remarked, taking another sip of wine.

I returned to my chaise lounge, sat down, giving Jack a serious, stern look. "Well, Sarah for one, and maybe mutual church friends for the other," I said gravely.

Without skipping a beat, Jack declared, "Oh, Amber Hardie, you are so silly. First of all, the church has better things to do with their money than to spend it on a private detective to catch us together. And secondly, Sarah would never do anything like that." Jack was confident and insistent in his position.

"How do *you* know?" I countered, unswayed by his argument.

"Because I know Sarah, and she would never do that." He was adamant in his assertion.

I leaned back for a moment. Then I acted on my theory. "Well, just in case, I am going to lock the screen doors," I said with a smirk.

Not wanting to appear too concerned, I used Jack's music to dance over to the first screen door on the left and locked it. Jack smiled, watching with ridiculous approval. Then, to further diffuse the situation, I danced past the pool and locked the screen door on the right. Jack just sat there laughing at my paranoia and my dancing abilities. I sat back down and placed my arm on his while looking into his eyes.

"There...much better!" I said, relieved.

Through Jack's deep laughter, he replied, "I am glad you are happy now. I didn't know you could dance like that!"

"I didn't either!" I said. "It must be the great music...or the wine!"

That made us both laugh out loud.

But we weren't laughing for long. To our grave surprise, at that moment Sarah unexpectedly appeared at the left screen door. Upon seeing the two of us sitting arm in arm, she froze in disbelief. She tried opening the door but, of course, couldn't. She continued jiggling the door in frustration. Jack got up to meet her while I sat immobilized in my lounge chair. I felt the blood drain from my face, and my legs went numb. Jack was extremely calm yet direct toward his wife.

"Sarah, what are you doing here? Don't do this. Just go."

Sarah, on the other hand, was not so calm, but became even louder upon hearing his request.

"Jack, open the door!" She was livid...and rightly so.

"Sarah, please. Just leave." Jack remained calm.

It was clear that Sarah was about to lose her temper. She began screaming, "Open this door, *now!*" Enraged, she then stomped her foot on the floor and started banging on the door.

"Sarah, don't do this. Please, just leave," Jack pleaded.

The blood now starting to return to my legs, I decided it best to use those legs to get out of there...*fast*. I quickly made my way into the house, not knowing what else to do. I was in a fog, not knowing what to do next. I didn't want Sarah to see my clothes hanging in the bedroom closet and my toiletries on the bathroom sink. I did not know where Sarah was parked and so was not sure if I could back out of the garage with her car in the driveway.

I wanted to sneak my personal belongings to the car so Sarah would not see them. However, the garage was on the opposite side of the house from the bedroom. I was fearful Sarah would see me running since the entire back of the house was in plain view of the open sliding glass doors. I could hear Sarah still screaming at Jack, and Jack trying to calm her down, but without success. I was a wreck and was perplexed as to what I should do. The guilt that lay beneath the surface suddenly came bursting into my conscience. I began trembling in fear of my horrific sin.

Frantically pacing in circles around the bedroom, I could hear the voices getting louder and closer. It was my worst nightmare come true. Then it got worse as Sarah came bursting into the house.

Jack had opened the screen door in an effort to calm Sarah and talk her down from her elevated emotional state, but by this time she was clearly out of control. Sarah came running in the bedroom and in a burning rage announced that she was going to kill me. Jack was right behind her and physically held her back. Sarah was trying to wrestle herself from Jack's grip and push him out of the way, all the while screaming at me. I was terrified and sobbing uncontrollably. While shouting, Sarah lifted her fists in the air, and had I taken a step forward, she would have surely knocked me out. As large as he is, Jack struggled to keep control of her. Sarah remained at the foot of the bed, continuing to scream at me over and over again, "I am going to kill you!"

I had never seen this side of Sarah and never imagined she could ever act this way. But then again, what woman wouldn't act this way when confronting the "other woman." All her anger seemed to fly past Jack and land directly on me. Jack was merely in the way, preventing her from reaching me.

Jack couldn't contain Sarah, and unless something happened fast, someone in that bedroom was going to get hurt. Jack looked at me and asked me to go. He knew he had a better chance of containing Sarah and calming her down if I were out of the house. I complied, and with only time enough to grab my purse and keys, I hastily ran to the car and opened the garage door. All the way there I could hear Sarah's haunting screams from the bedroom.

"I'm going to kill you!"

Fortunately, she had parked in the circular driveway, leaving plenty of room for me to pull out of the garage. Backing up my car, I wondered if she had intentionally left me an open avenue of escape. I was shaking so hard, I wondered if I could make the hour trip home. I managed to drive down to the local grocery store parking lot where I pulled in and parked in order to breathe and calm down. Turning off the engine, I sat there and cried for what seemed like hours.

This horrifying event filled me with fear and anguish. And there was nowhere to turn. No person to tell. After all, who could I call? Who could I tell? Who could I confide in? No one I know would condone my situation or sympathize with me. And besides, no one knew what I was doing. At least that's what I thought.

My double life of lies had woven a web of deceit, trapping me and wrapping around me like a cocoon. I was out on a limb all by myself. Sitting in that parking lot, I wondered what was going on back at the house. How was I going to get my belongings? I wondered if Jack was okay.

My thoughts then turned to all our church friends finding out about our situation. I imagined the further pain this would cause my son. I sat weeping for hours, horrified at what my life had become. I tried to pray, but how could I? What could I possibly say? I was wrong, and I knew it. It wasn't just the sinful choices or the sinful life I had lived. I began to see more clearly that *I* was the real problem. *I* had made all those choices. And now here I was. A well-known proverb repeated in my mind, "You can choose your sin, but you cannot choose your consequences." I was now reaping what I had sown these many months.

After hours of sitting paralyzed in my car, my phone rang. With trembling hands, I fumbled to answer it. Quivering, I answered, "Hello?"

I was relieved to hear Jack's voice.

"Are you okay, Amber?" Jack asked with a calm, quiet voice.

"Yes," I whispered quickly, still gasping for air.

"Good. I am glad you are okay. Sarah would like to talk to you."
Wait. What? Sarah? I thought. *She's there? With Jack? Still?*

Jack said Sarah wanted to apologize to me. But the only thing I could think was, *Sarah wants to apologize to me? I'm the one who should be apologizing to her, not the other way around. Is this for real? Is this really happening?*

My heart sank as Jack handed the phone to Sarah. She came on and through her soft, weeping voice she pleaded, "Amber, I am sorry for the harsh words I spoke to you and the way I reacted. Will you forgive me?"

I was dumbfounded and confused. This was surreal, making me feel like I was in the middle of a bad dream. *Just a while ago she was determined to kill me, and now she is apologizing to me?*

I somehow temporarily regained my composure. "Sarah, you don't...you don't..." I tried forming a sentence as I cried back to Sarah. "You don't have to be sorry. *I* am the one who is sorry for being there with Jack. You had every right to be mad."

I couldn't imagine what Jack had said to calm Sarah down. How in the world did he persuade Sarah to ask me for forgiveness? How did he twist Sarah's mind into thinking she was at fault and needed to ask for forgiveness? After all I would have surely acted the same way had I found my husband with another woman. Sarah was right, and I was wrong.

Through my ongoing tears and pain, I managed a whisper. "Please forgive *me*, Sarah." My weeping hindered my ability to speak. Swallowing, I managed to utter these words. "I am so sorry for hurting you."

Sarah spoke like her usual calm, sweet self. "Yes, Amber, I forgive you. But will you forgive me too?"

Still dismayed at her asking me that, I replied. "Yes, Sarah, of course."

Sarah was kind, quick, and to the point. "Thank you, Amber. Good-bye."

I just looked at my phone, wondering, *What just happened here?*

*****

Jack and Sarah had talked for hours while I sat in that grocery store parking lot crying my eyes out. This dramatic incident prompted Jack to go back home again to smooth things over and calm Sarah down. I thought of the many times Jack had said if we were "discovered," it would expedite his divorce. So much for that theory. His own wife had found us together, and now Jack was going back home with her…again.

Jack and Sarah were in two separate cars as they drove back to their Palm Beach home. The hour drive back gave Jack the opportunity to call me from his car. I was still crying but managed a meek, "Hello?"

Jack was calm and caring, yet frustrated. "Amber, are you okay?" He spoke in his deep, soft voice that I yearned to hear.

"Where are you?"

Just hearing his voice always made me melt.

Without waiting for me to answer, he softly asked, "What are you doing?"

I didn't know where or how to begin. My thoughts were like a pendulum, swinging back and forth between "It's over" to "I love you." My heart was swirling with pain, hurt, sorrow, and turmoil. Four hours later my body was still frozen, sitting in my car in a lonely grocery store parking lot.

Jack broke the silence with his self-confident voice. "Amber… are…you…okay?"

I gathered what little strength I had, replying, "I am in the Publix parking lot, down the street from your home. I have been sitting here this whole time trying to figure out what to do. Wondering what was going on and if you were okay." I hesitated for a moment, realizing that is not what Jack was expecting to hear. "I am fine." I paused, realizing I had just lied to him. I decided to be honest. "No, no…I am not fine. How can I be fine?"

Jack quickly recognized I was an emotional wreck and interrupted me in his deep, calm voice. "Amber, I am so sorry. Please try to calm down." Jack could hear me sniffling, and I could tell it broke his heart. He knew I was losing it. I decided to remain silent.

"Amber, I need to go home for a while. It took some time, but I was able to calm Sarah down. I do not want to upset her any more than she is already. And I definitely do not want her going home and telling anyone what happened today. I know how devastating that would be to you. I don't want this to hurt you beyond what you've already experienced. I believe if I go home for a while, Sarah will keep this incident just between us. I know that is what is best for you. I know how private you are, and I am trying to respect that."

I had no words, but just listened.

"Amber, I don't know how long this is going to take. Sarah promised to keep quiet if I go home. So, as much as I don't want to, I am going home because I think this is what is best for you." Jack still did not hear any words from me, and only the sniffling sound assured him I was still on the line.

"Amber, I think it will be best for you to go back to the house and remove all your belongings, just in case. I don't want you to be dragged deeper into this situation. Most of our shared friends think that I have separated from Sarah because of our mutual differences. I don't want you to be incriminated into this situation."

I remained silent, processing all this information.

"Amber, can you do that? Just use the garage code and pull into the garage. Load up your car and then lock the garage. This way you will be safe from feeling any further conviction here."

I was still unable to reason, and I also couldn't help thinking who Jack was protecting from feeling convicted here—me or himself. So many questions were floating in my head. So I asked the most troubling question first. "How did you get Sarah to apologize to me?" There was silence, so I rephrased my question, "Why did Sarah apologize to me?"

"Amber, Sarah was clearly upset when she saw us together. Her reaction was an emotional explosion. After I calmed her down, we spoke about the way she treated you and the threatening words she spoke. She realized her reaction was mean-spirited and evil. I believe if I had not been able to hold her back from you, she would have done you harm. Sarah was broken at her overreaction and what she may have been capable of doing. She wanted to apologize to clear her own heart and conscience," he said confidently.

His explanation sounded reasonable enough, filtered through my emotionally-charged state of mind.

"How long are you going to be home with her?" I asked.

Jack was slow to answer the question but quick to start talking. "Amber, I want to protect you as best I can. I don't want anyone else to find out about this. I do not want to ruin your reputation, and I do not want to hurt Joshua and Shanna with this situation. I know how much they love you and how they are concerned about your well-being." He hesitated. "Amber, I am not sure how long I will stay home. That is why I want you to go back to the house and get everything you need. I will stay home just as long as it takes to calm Sarah down so she won't talk about this."

I thought that sounded reasonable too. Searching for more questions, my next question was what I had wondered the last few hours. "Did Sarah look around the house and see my stuff?"

Jack answered quickly, "No, I kept her in the den and we sat on the couch. I made her some tea, and we talked there for hours while I calmed her down. She never looked around the house. I had her freshen up in the guest bathroom. Once she was calm, I walked her out to her car. She never gazed or searched, I promise. After we spoke, she left quietly."

Hearing Jack's deep voice calmed me. All this was still more than I could bear. With regret and sorrow filling my voice, I said, "Jack, I have been sitting here thinking for hours. I think we should just end this relationship. I cannot continue like this. I never wanted to enter into this relationship while you were still married."

I hesitated, and for the first time since I had known him, Jack was speechless. I began to cry but continued talking as best I could.

"I will go back to the house and get my belongings...but please do not call me until you are officially divorced."

"Amber, I knew this would upset you. Please remember I am doing this for you. I love you, and promise we will be together soon. Just give me some time. I promise, when this smoke clears, we will be together," he said.

He was obviously concerned about what this now meant for our relationship. He was worried this episode would get back to our church friends and family and how it would create even more problems for me. Jack told me he didn't care about himself as he had already resigned his membership at the church and no one there would bother him. However, I now had more to risk and lose with our church friends. Before hanging up, Jack made sure I would go back and get my belongings. He made it clear that neither one of us would go back to the Fort Lauderdale home for an indefinite period of time.

We spoke for almost an hour during his ride home. He continued explaining how Sarah was an emotional mess and that he needed to go home for a while.

After making sure the coast was clear, I went back inside the house on the water and emptied it of all my belongings. And though Jack said Sarah did not look around the house or notice any of my belongings there, I had my doubts. Sometimes we choose what to see. Sometimes we choose what we want to believe.

*****

Amazingly, this recent episode didn't reach our church family and friends. It should have leaked, sparked, and spread like wildfire; but it didn't. Instead, a more palatable story began spreading around. It was a story of how Jack and Sarah were back together and trying to patch things up. Sarah had been so happy to have him back that she did not tell anyone about the situation at the Fort Lauderdale home.

So now I was back to square one. Jack was home again; and I was back seeking more forgiveness, mercy, and grace. I felt terrible, emotionally and spiritually buried under conviction and embarrassment. Jack and I had finally decided to stay apart until he was legally divorced. Once again I went through the holidays alone, another lonely Christmas and another tearful New Year's Eve. Once again I attempted to get my life back on track. I tried to seek God, but with all the wrong motives. I wanted God, and I went back to church, and once again swore we would not be together until Jack was legally divorced.

As I had requested, Jack and I did not see each other, though Jack continued with phone calls and e-mails. The pain of us being apart was overwhelming, and by the beginning of February, Jack again broke away from Sarah and moved back down to the Fort Lauderdale home. This time he told Sarah it was a permanent move, and much to her dismay, he actually began divorce proceedings.

26

Obfuscation

My phone rang, and I immediately reached for it, suspecting it was Jack. However, to my surprise, it was from a woman named Donna who attended my church. Donna and her husband were close friends with Sarah and Jack, and she was also one of the ladies Bible study teachers. She said she wanted to ask me some questions regarding my line of work and how my firm might be able to help her family. Pretty straightforward.

We met at Starbucks, casually chatting over coffee. I informed her about the available services in town that could help her family situation. Donna was a kind, gentle lady who embodied character and integrity. Her intense relationship with God and her gift of making the Bible come alive motivated people to flock to the Bible study classes she held.

After gathering all the information she needed, she then turned to me and bluntly said, "Now let's talk about Jack and Sarah Hardie."

Ah, there it was, the *real* reason for the visit, the hidden motive behind our chat. I felt tricked. Deceived. Donna met me at Starbucks under false pretenses, and that made my blood boil. Evidently, Sarah had been confiding in Donna and now she was coming to Sarah's defense.

What right does she have to do this to me? What right does she have to corner me this way? I felt ambushed and blindsided. And my sinful heart reared its ugly head as I went on the defense.

"Oh, what about Jack and Sarah Hardie?" I calmly replied. I was furious but tried to keep a serene and confident exterior.

Donna was direct, cutting right through my smoke screen and getting straight to the point. "I understand you are in an inappropriate relationship with Jack."

Now it was time for me to bring out the big guns. If Donna was going to be this direct, then I would be equally evasive. I went into obfuscation mode, dodging my way around the conversation.

"I don't know what you are talking about. Jack and I are good friends," I said, nonchalantly taking a sip of my latte.

Oh, I was good. I had been trained by the best, Jack having taught me well. In fact, so convinced our relationship was justified, I believe that day I could have passed a lie detector test. Jack was so unhappy, and being a wonderful man, he *deserved* happiness. And Sarah deserved someone who loved her as well. So yes, I believed our relationship was legitimate.

Unfazed, Donna then launched into her concerns about what Sarah had revealed to her. She knew about the gold-and-diamond necklace Christmas present, the car accident, and about Sarah catching Jack and I together at the Fort Lauderdale waterfront house. And yet Donna's tone wasn't accusatory or condemning. She didn't point any self-righteous fingers at me either. Rather, she merely brought up what she had heard from Sarah and asked if it was true. She was as calm as I was, only her composure flowed from a peaceful, godly reputation, not deception and self-preservation as mine had.

I held it together pretty good throughout the conversation, pretending that it really wasn't that serious. I explained that it was merely a case of others exaggerating our relationship. I did, however, throw her a bone, admitting to an inappropriate "friendship." I insisted that it was over and done with. So there was no smoking gun here and no evidence to convict me in the court of public opinion—

that is, unless someone dug deeper. But although I had been living a secret double life, I was not about to crack under this lightweight interrogation.

I later discovered that when Jack left Sarah again and returned to the Fort Lauderdale home, she decided the time for keeping quiet was over. She had become increasingly more verbal about her husband's relationship with me, confiding in our mutual circle of church friends.

Our coffee cups were now empty, and Donna seemed satisfied with my version of the story. But before leaving, she did offer some counsel, encouraging me to sever any relationship I may currently have with Jack and that I cut off any form of communication I might have with him, whether through phone calls, e-mails, or personally seeing him. I assured her I would, lying through my teeth. Donna also warned me of the effects of sin and adultery. Then she prayed with me, and we left.

Leaving Starbucks that day, I was furious that I had been lured there under false pretenses and that she had played "counselor" to me. But I was equally angry with myself for meeting Donna in the first place. By the time I reached my car, I was an emotional mess. And yet, as infuriated as I was with Donna, I knew deep in my heart that she was doing the right thing. Out of all our mutual church friends, Donna was the only person with the spiritual maturity and courage to confront me. And yet I now believe she did it with love and kindness and to try and make a difference in my life.

Only she was willing to enter the spiritual battle on my behalf. Instead of hammering me with guilt and shame, she wisely allowed the Holy Spirit room to work in my heart and life.

I called Jack right away and told him what happened. Like me, he was also furious that Donna had cornered me and that Sarah was now seeking people to "help" her. Although I pretended that Donna's confrontation did not bother me, deep down it plagued my heart and conscience. Donna's words echoed over and over in my head for weeks to come. God was using Donna to impart some light and wisdom into my dark and broken life. But I wasn't budging.

Because of my anger with Donna for confronting me, I even spoke badly about her to our mutual acquaintances. My heart was so dulled by my sin that I was lashing out at whoever got in my way. For her part, Donna had no idea of the effect she had on me and the way her words cut into my hard heart day after day. God was slowly chipping away at me, but I was still too blind to see. I was caught in the epicenter of a heated spiritual battle, and I was totally unaware at the forces that waged warfare both for me and against me. All I knew was to run for comfort…and cover. So I headed to our retreat house in Fort Lauderdale.

*****

However, once back there, my life just wasn't the same. I grew extremely self-conscious and frightened of getting caught with Jack again. The pain of my guilt became almost unbearable as I began thinking of how much sorrow Sarah must be feeling. And yet, even with this constant mental anguish and soul agony, I refused to break.[11]

This sin-induced sorrow and suffering was putting a real strain on my relationship with Jack. He wanted me there all the time, and I hardly ever wanted to come, making every excuse to leave early or simply to stay home. I didn't want to go out in public with him. I was tired of being the "*other* woman," even though Jack promised me that I was the "*only* woman." We stopped going to our favorite restaurants for my fear of getting caught. We stopped playing tennis and going swimming. We no longer went out to shoot pool or go to our favorite pub to throw darts because I felt like we were being followed. I was paranoid, and as a result, Jack was upset at me, though he did try to understand.

---

[11] Beth Moore describes it this way: "The power of seduction is indescribable, however. Not inescapable, nor totally irresistible, but indescribable. If you've never been hit by a satanic tidal wave, you're inclined to think that walking away from any sin is a matter of making a simple decision. You may never have experienced the feeling of being completely overpowered. Again, we see that Satan's attempt is to inspire a feeling so strong it eclipses the truth." Ibid, 44.

So in light of my uneasiness concerning the Fort Lauderdale home, we started traveling together. We ventured to other beaches further south, taking trips to the Florida Keys. We still took the time to watch the sunset far from our "home." We took long rides, traveling to far away towns and hotels. We were trying our combined best to live life together; but our sin, fear, and shame were slowly drowning the relationship.

27

A Secret Wife?

Jack loved shopping, and he was great at it. Few things gave him more satisfaction than choosing and buying clothes and accessories for me. Whenever we were at our favorite department store, he was like a little boy in a candy store. He became my personal shopper, insisting I try on all the new styles. While I was in the dressing room trying something on I had picked out, Jack would go fetch a different size, color, or style. Every time he came back with twice as much. And that Saturday was no different.

"Look what I found, Amber. This would look great on you," he said.

"But I don't really need that, Jack."

"Oh, just try it on. You could always wear it somewhere."

"Okay, but it better be on sale." Even though Jack always paid the bill, I hated paying full price for something that would go on sale next week.

"Don't start with me again," he jokingly argued. "I told you, when it goes on sale they run out of sizes and the best colors. If you want something nice, you have to get it *before* it goes on sale. I just want you to have the best, Amber. I want you to have the styles you want before the store runs out of merchandise."

He was running back and forth, trying to find just the right clothes for me. After successfully accomplishing his mission, he went searching for shoes and accessories, bringing them back to me with such delight.

*****

One day after work I went home to rest and recharge. But upon walking through the door, something seemed strange. There was a cup on the kitchen countertop I knew I didn't place there. Suspicious, I began looking around the house. Then I noticed my desk drawer was slightly open. I continued roaming the house and saw that the bathroom door was slightly closed. I found this odd as I usually left it open all the way. Slowly ascending the stairs, I wondered if I was imagining these things.

Arriving at my bedroom, I spotted on top of the dresser a shopping bag and three shoeboxes. Peering inside the bag, I spotted a receipt. Picking it up, I scanned to the bottom where I saw the amount spent on these gifts. Opening each box of shoes, I, of course, loved them. How could I not? My personal shopper had hand selected each of them just for me. Grabbing my phone, I immediately called Jack.

"Hello," he answered in a deep, soft voice that rumbled like quiet thunder.

"Hi, Jack. Do you have something to tell me?"

"I don't think so. Why?" he said, chuckling. "Where are you?"

"I am home. Where are you?"

He answered quickly, "I'm at home too."

"What did you do today?" I asked. I could tell he was being playful.

"Well, you know, a little of this and a little of that."

I played back. "Did 'a little of this and a little of that' include driving to West Palm Beach today?"

"Why do you ask?" he snickered.

"Well, there are three brand-new pairs of shoes in my bedroom that weren't here when I left this morning," I replied.

"You're kidding me!" he remarked in a serious tone. "Someone broke into your house?"

"Well, no forced entry, just new shoes."

"Well, that's funny…a burglar that brings you stuff rather than taking it," he declared, laughing.

"Oh, Jack. You are unbelievable," I gratefully replied. "Why did you come all the way here to bring me shoes?"

He paused for a minute and then answered matter-of-factly. "Amber, you told me your feet were hurting you the other day while you were at work. I just want you to be comfortable. Those dress shoes are guaranteed to be comfortable, or you can return them. I love you, Amber. I only want to make you happy."

His kindness melted my heart, as he knew exactly how to break down my defenses. And even though I was planning on staying home a few days, I changed my mind. Unable to resist the urge, I drove to the house in Fort Lauderdale to be with Jack.

*****

We just loved each other and looked forward to the day when we could finally be together for life. I still believed Jack when he said, "Love is what you do, not what you say."

However, I was noticing little things about him that began making me uncomfortable. Instead of obfuscating others, he seemed to be obfuscating *me*. I wasn't sure if it was my suspicious nature or if perhaps I was making a bigger deal out of things than I should.

It began when I decided to look at Jack's e-mail account. Much to my surprise, he had been receiving e-mails from Chen, and evidently, they had been "talking." But not only was he receiving e-mails from Chen, I then discovered that when Jack and Chen were together, Chen had actually taken on his last name. She signed her e-mails "Chen Hardie." I knew she had been anticipating his permanent return to her country, but I did not know she had taken on his last name. When I read, "Chen Hardie," I wanted to throw up.

Since Jack did not know I had read the e-mail, I casually asked him if he had heard from Chen. Thankfully, he was honest and told me she had contacted him. But to my dismay, he also said that since she was such a kind and gentle person, he felt like he would always need to be in touch with her. Chen was a poor, handicapped young woman, and Jack felt some obligation should he need to help her in the future. He also said that since I was also such a kind and gentle person, he was sure I would understand. I was taken by surprise at this statement. And quite frankly, it made me sick.

I did not respond right away as I wanted to give Jack a reasonable, well thought-out response. Jack Hardie was a retired oil salesman who could sell ice in the Arctic. Having run a major corporation, he was now the owner and CEO of one of the largest real estate firms in Florida (although semiretired from that too). He had a way of spinning conversations around, obfuscating the real issue.

I thought, *Could this be how he got Sarah to apologize to me? What exactly did he say to her that would make her turn around and apologize to me when she discovered me together with her husband?*

I had to think through the Chen scenario. Could I live knowing Jack was talking to a former love, even though she was halfway around the world and no real threat to me? After all I was convinced Jack loved me and that we were destined to be together. And he was right about one thing, I really am a kind and gentle person, maybe even too much so sometimes.

After contemplating the situation, I decided I was unwilling to live knowing he was still connected to a former love interest. No matter how much he loved me or how much I loved him, to me it was an unacceptable proposition and I wouldn't stand for it under any circumstances. On second thought, maybe I wasn't as kind and gentle as Jack thought I was.

A few days later I sat Jack down and had a serious talk with him, explaining my feelings about Chen. I told him how I didn't believe it was right for him to hold on to their relationship, no matter how far away it was. Not to mention the fact that Chen was even younger than I was. Jack seemed a bit taken aback with my conclusion but agreed nonetheless.

"Amber, you too have a vote in our relationship, and I choose to honor your vote. I will stop e-mailing Chen if it bothers you that much."

I had my doubts whether he would honor my "vote"; however, I sincerely wanted to believe he was telling me the truth. Sometimes we choose to believe only what we want to believe.

*****

During this time, there were other little things that I was noticing about Jack, though I routinely attributed them to my suspicious nature. After all Jack was still loving, kind, and generous as ever. He could not do enough wonderful things for me—showering me with presents, cooking wonderful meals, and expressing his undying love in numerous creative and romantic ways.

However, since I wasn't living there with him, he was also going out more in the evenings. He always told me where he was going and called to say good night when he got home. I was not comfortable with him being out at night, but I was also not ready to return and live at the Fort Lauderdale house anymore. But it didn't really matter as I figured that in a short time, we would be together permanently.

In May I went back to Boston for my daughter Stephanie's birthday and to spend a long weekend with her and her husband, after which I planned to see Rachel and her husband. Jack was all in favor of my trip and excited for me to have relaxing time with my girls. The night before I left Jack cooked a delicious candlelight dinner for us. After the meal I told Jack I could not stay the night as I had a lot to get done before leaving for the long weekend.

It was difficult for me to relax at the house as I expected Sarah to show up again at any moment. And this, as I had previously discovered, was definitely not unreasonable paranoia. But at this point, any excuse was a good excuse for me. I couldn't stay there. Though Jack knew how unnerving it was to me, he repeatedly told me I was overreacting.

I successfully left that evening instead of staying the night, but Jack was not happy with me. And for the first time in our relationship, he even seemed a bit perturbed with me, expressing his disapproval for my decision and his need for me to stay. I reiterated my need for his divorce to be finalized as I could not cope with another confrontation with Sarah.

While I was away in Boston, we spoke every morning and every evening. Although Jack sent e-mails and text messages expressing his unwavering love and devotion, when we talked there was something in his voice that I found unsettling. Jack would tell me half-truths that kept me wondering if I was getting the whole story. This was his way of telling on himself.

That Saturday night I called Jack to check in with him.

"Hi, Jack."

"Hi, my love," he said in his deep sexy voice.

"What did you do today?" I inquired.

He answered quietly, "Well, nothing much. Just stayed home." Then his voice picked up a bit. "I did go swimming today."

"Swimming? What do you mean you went swimming? You hate the pool."

Jack never swam unless it was very hot. And even then I had to practically force him into the pool.

"Well, I figured while you were away I would go swimming," he announced. "I know how much you love the pool, so I am trying to get used to it...for you."

"Oh, well, that's sweet," I said, feeling uneasy about his answer. I felt guilty for my lack of trust. "What else did you do today?"

He thought for a minute and then responded. "Well, I cooked dinner," he said proudly.

"You what? You hate to cook!" I reminded him. I had taught Jack how to cook, but he only did so when I was by his side. He never cooked for himself.

"I am practicing for when you get home, Amby. I want to be a good cook for you," he said with a quiet, confident rumble. He made me feel guilty again.

I couldn't quite put my finger on it, but I just knew something was not right.

It was at this point that God began untying the blindfolds.

28

A Look in the Mirror

When I got back to Palm Beach, I immediately went straight to the home in Fort Lauderdale. I missed Jack so much and was so glad to see him. For his part he was as loving and attentive as ever and excited for me to be home. We had a nice romantic dinner together complete with dimmed lighting, flowers, and candles...as usual. Jack was a fast learner and had perfected his cooking abilities, proudly showing them off to me while I watched. After this delicious dinner, I helped Jack clean the kitchen and wash, dry, and put away all the dishes. Then we cuddled up to watch a movie complete with fresh-made popcorn. I was feeling terrible for my earlier insecurities and suspicions.

The next morning, we drove to our favorite restaurant for a big breakfast. Then we went back to the house to talk about the future, relax, watch TV, and cuddle all afternoon. Our conversations were legendary, lasting hours. Jack's warm embrace and soft fragrance was irresistible. I left late that afternoon to go home to West Palm Beach and regroup after my long trip. Pulling out of the garage, I blasted one of our favorite Josh Groban songs on the car stereo, "As You

Say You Love Me." Jack stood silently in the garage with a big smile and bright blue eyes, waving good-bye. He looked so handsome in his pressed blue jeans and Ralph Lauren shirt. I was thrilled that I stopped there first before going home.

*****

However, that evening something deeply troubled me. I tried calling Jack a number of times but to no avail. This was strange, as he always answered his phone. I tried to tell myself I was overreacting, that I was being silly. The spiritual battle for my life was heating up. That day God stepped out of heaven and wrestled for my heart and life, although I was oblivious to it at the time.

I kept thinking I should go back to the Fort Lauderdale house, but it was an hour away. I wondered, *What would I say to Jack? That I was just passing by the neighborhood? How could I tell him the truth, that I was having insecurities about our relationship?*

I knew that if I merely drove there to check up on him and tell him what I was feeling, he would remind me that I chose not to live there with him while he proceeded with the divorce. And by seeking the divorce, he would say that he was proving his love to me with his *actions. "Love is what you do…not what you say."* The last time I raised the issue of my insecurity to him, he said, *"Have you forgotten? You are the love of my life. Look at all I am doing for you!"*

Finally, as I was getting in bed, Jack called. He apologized for not answering the phone but explained that he had forgotten to turn it on. It was a quick good night, and we hung up. And yet I couldn't shake the feeling. My intuition told me something was just not right. I tried to go to bed but instead tossed and turned all night long. My stomach was upset, and I cried all night as my mind raced with all types of scenarios. Of course, other than my feelings, I had nothing tangible to go on. The spiritual war within me was in full force, with my spiritual and emotional bondage tearing me apart.

Since I couldn't sleep anyway, I got up early the next morning, took a shower, and got dressed. I decided I would go to the Fort Lauderdale retreat house at sunrise to surprise Jack. At the very least, it would be a surprise visit to tell him how much I missed him and loved him. At the very worst, my suspicions and fears would be confirmed.

That hour drive seemed like two, I felt sick to my stomach and extremely nervous of making a fool of myself. My mind began racing again, *What would he think if he knew I was being so insecure? What if Sarah was there? What would I say then?*

I called Jack's phone just as I approached the house to see if I could wake him up and get some kind of clue as to the situation, but there was no answer. I called again. Still no answer. Pulling into the driveway, my heart skipped a beat. I parked, and as I got out of the car, my legs buckled.

I decided to knock instead of using my key. I didn't know why I wanted to knock. I just did. Within a few seconds, Jack walked up and looked through the see-through glass entrance door. He was wearing just his underwear.

"Amber, w-what are you doing here? I just got your message, and I was about to call you."

His phone was in his hand. Then he pointed to the doorknob while signaling through the glass pane. "Wait there while I get the key to the door." He then turned and went back into the bedroom. I wondered why he said that, leaving me standing there outside. This was odd as the spare key was always right there in a tray on the ledge, right by the front door in case of an emergency.

My heart pounded, and my stomach turned. I felt my legs grow weak. *What am I going to say? What am I going to do?* I had no idea what I was doing. I was just taking it one step at a time. I had no clue what was going on around me in the spiritual realm or how God was using this moment in the battle for my soul.

Jack soon returned to the glass door, still in his underwear, claiming he could not find the key. He signaled to me that he was going to let me in through the garage. I proceeded to leave the stoop and began walking around to the garage. The first thing I thought was that since he wanted me to walk through the garage, there must not be another car in there. That was a good sign. I began to feel really guilty about my mistrust of Jack, and thought, *Now what should I do?*

Jack opened the garage, still dressed only in his underwear. I entered in through the garage and into the kitchen. The garage, kitchen, and den were on one side of the house with the master bedroom on the other.

Walking through the kitchen, I noticed two dinner dishes, two wine glasses, two water glasses, and an array of utensils still drying by the kitchen sink. My heart rate instantly soared, and I felt my blood begin to boil.

Jack asked me to sit down in the den, on the couch. I glanced at the couch with apprehension, then looked back at him. I sat down hesitantly, in the same way I had sat two years earlier. Why I sat, I really didn't know. My mind was a confusing intersection jammed with all kinds of thoughts, none of which were good. Jack sat on the couch next to me as he rubbed his hands on my shoulders. Now my heart began beating even faster.

He looked right into my eyes, gently pushing the black curls off my face while caressing my shoulders. Parting my bangs to better see my eyes, he half-smiled. "I...I am so glad to see you, Amber girl. What are you doing here?" Still only wearing his underwear, he was almost naked as we sat there on the couch together. He seemed a bit preoccupied, yet still his usual tender and sweet self.

"I wanted to surprise you," I said, my voice now shaking with fear. I was still uncertain of my suspicions. His mantra, "Love is what you *do*, not what you *say*?" reverberated in my head. I hesitated, taking a deep breath. That's when I felt tears beginning to form. "Well, I wanted to surprise you and show you how much I love you." I don't know what made me say that. I don't even know how I got that out of my mouth as my entire body was now shaking in disbelief.

"What a nice surprise...can I make you a cup of tea?"

I swallowed deeply to hold back the tears. "No, thank you," I said apprehensively as we looked into each other's eyes. His bright blue eyes had somehow faded.

"Can I make you some breakfast?" He now seemed to be scrambling for something to say.

I choked and tried to talk, but only a whisper escaped. "No, thank you."

I felt paralyzed, frozen in a cocktail of confusion mixed with suspicion, fear, and anger. It took every ounce of energy I had to break free from his warm embrace, endearing words, and powerful control.

"I need to use the bathroom…it was a long ride," I said, jolting up from the couch. I needed to turn away before I burst into tears.

Jack swiftly jumped to his feet and attempted to divert my attention to the hallway bathroom off the kitchen. "Amber, use *this* bathroom."

I could tell, perhaps for the first time in his life, he was struggling to maintain control of a situation. I never used that hallway bathroom. My bathroom was located off the master bedroom. It was a large bathroom with a wide shower, extra-large tub, and his and her sinks. My sink was on the left side and his on the right side. He knew that.

I stopped in my tracks as I suddenly recalled how Jack told me he had kept Sarah in the den so she wouldn't see anything in the bedroom. I quickly turned to look at him. "No, thank you. I want to use my bathroom so I can freshen up."

My heart was now aching with grave trepidation, unsure of what I would find. Jack's face became ashen, confused as to what he should do next. I continued my bold walk through the kitchen, living room, the dining room, and on into the bedroom. Passing the front door, I caught a glimpse of the door key on the tray by the ledge. Right where it always was.

Jack was trailing close behind me.

"Amber, please stop. Amber…Amber! Please do not go in there." His voice was stern but pregnant with panic.

I kept on walking.

The bedroom door was shut as I placed a trembling hand on the doorknob. Turning it, I pushed it open to discover a bleached-blond, spiked-haired woman in Jack's bed, crouching under the covers. I walked right up to the side of the bed to get a better look at this strange woman.

Jack was right behind me crying, "I'm sorry, my Amber…I am so sorry!"

There are times in life when people seem to act outside their bodies and minds. This was one of those moments for me. Maybe it wasn't me at all. Maybe, just maybe, it was God speaking through me…and, oddly enough, to me as well.

I glared at this woman, lying where I once slept. The levels of hurt, pain, and disgust overflowed within me. Once again I heard my own words, this time with a barbed edge.

"Did he tell you he was married?"

No sooner did those words leave my mouth that they boomeranged back toward me. It was as if my own words of condemnation toward this one-night stand were turning against me. Looking down at the scantily-clad blonde, my words became a firing squad of truth penetrating my very heart and soul. I was looking into a full-length mirror, looking at myself! *She is me! I am her!* Was the only difference between the two of us the duration of his deception? I was receiving the due recompense of my own horrific offense. I was now standing on the other side of the pain and anguish.

Ironically, I was standing in the very spot Sarah stood when she screamed she was going to kill me. The blonde was frozen under the covers, and I was frozen for words…and for what to do next. I quickly concluded, *What right do I have to do anything…or to say anything to this woman? When Sarah left town many years ago, Jack began to call me and I responded. When I left town, he simply called someone else. And she responded. She was the new "me."*

Then to my utmost surprise, the bleach-blond girl under the covers answered me.

"Yes…he told me that he was married," she said in an unforgettable deep, husky voice.

That was it. I had no more words. I wondered, *Does she think I am his wife? Who does she think I am?* Then I realized it didn't really matter. I stood there utterly dismayed, deeply hurt, and thoroughly guilty. I managed to temporarily regain my composure, then turned around and marched out of the room. I realized I had no right to ask her that question, and the grave reality sunk into me for the first time. I had no rights. No right to him. No right to question. No right to judge. The "other woman" has no ground upon which to stand.

She simply rolls the dice and hopes for a favorable outcome. That's it. It's a life gamble that makes anything in Vegas pale in comparison. I had rolled the dice for two years, thinking I was on a winning streak and cheating the odds. In reality I was only raising the stakes with every meal, every trip, every walk on the beach, every sunset, and every intimate moment with Jack. And with one final roll, I lost it all.

House wins.

I had tiptoed through the minefield for so long, thinking I was somehow immune to disaster. I had dodged the raindrops that had stained others. My past had been chasing me…and gaining on me. But I shrugged it off. When I first met Jack, I was merely "Amber." And now in that bedroom I was now the jilted lover. I had planted seeds of sin and misery thinking I would somehow reap a harvest of love and happiness. I had become too deceived to realize that whatever a person sows, that's what they will reap.

All at once my earthly existence collided with the spiritual realm, and the impact was pure devastation. My past—disgrace, sin, shame. My present—pain, hurt, torture, and heartache. And my future, as far as I could see—*gone*.

The reality of what I had become was excruciating.

I marched eagerly toward the garage, certain I was going to faint at any second. I wished I could just vomit up the foreboding sense of dread within me and be done with it.

Jack followed at my heels. "Amber, I'm sorry. I'm so sorry. She doesn't mean anything to me. Please forgive me."

He was crying with his hands on his head.

She doesn't mean anything to me? Was that supposed to make me feel better? Well, Jack, since she doesn't mean anything to you, that's a whole different story. No worries. It's really no big deal. Why don't we go back inside? I think I will have that breakfast now. In fact, why don't we ask blondie to join us!

*****

For the first time in the four years we had known each other, we exchanged harsh words and fought. I was leaving as Jack paced in circles, crying about how sorry he was.

This was a defining moment in my heart and life. The explosion of my sin's reality finally blew off my blindfolds and the scales on my eyes began to fall away. The battle was now in full force. For the first time Jack Hardie did not look like the groomed man of character and integrity I had always fantasized him to be. Standing there in his underwear, tears streaming down his cheeks, Jack now looked mean and dirty. No longer the confident, gallant gentleman and spiritual leader, the man in that house was revealed to be nothing more than a lying deceiver and weakling.

My eyes were opened; and my mind started recalling his past actions, events, stories, and lies. How could I be so stupid? I knew about the extramarital affairs throughout his marriage. I knew about Nyri and Chen. I knew how he taught me to *obfuscate*. I knew how he lied to Sarah. And I knew how he was involved with me. And yet I believed all along that I was different. *We* were different. But now I thought, *Why would I be any different? I am simply the "next girl."* The chipping away at my rock-encrusted heart was excruciating.

Reaching the door leading into the garage, I stopped in my tracks to face Jack. The time for mere harsh words was over. Instead, I said things to him that had never came out of my mouth before, calling him names I would never call my worst enemy. Then I did something I had never done to anyone in my life. I began punching him in his chest. Hard. Over and over I pelted him with my fists, crying, "How could you do this to me? I gave up everything for you. My family, my friends, my self-respect, my life as I once knew it, everything I once believed in." I continued slugging him with all the strength my tiny frame could muster as tears flowed incessantly from my eyes.

Jack did nothing in response. He just kept backing up with sorrow and shock on his face.

"You said you loved me," I shouted. "You said we were going to be together. You said we would make this relationship right. You said you would never hurt me. You said I could trust you. You said you would never leave me. You said 'love is what you do, not what you say.'" I looked toward the bedroom, pointing. "And *this*? This is what you do?" I kept hitting him in the chest.

Our relationship had begun with his gentle hands on my heart, and now it was ending with my furious fists pounding his. Jack's hand on my heart was his seduction, luring me in. My fists on his chest was my liberation, freeing me from this sinful spell I was under.

Jack grabbed my two hands, holding them tight against his chest, trying to gain control. His bright blue eyes were now darkened with pain as he peered right into my tear-soaked eyes and face stained with makeup. He then placed his hands on my shoulders to keep me still.

With an anguished voice he tearfully cried out, "Amber, I love you!" He began to reach for my curly black hair to move it away from my face as he had done countless times before. But I pulled away. He grabbed my head in his hands, locking eyes with me. He attempted to wipe the makeup and tears from my eyes as I tried to wiggle free. Before Jack could go any farther, I pulled away, gasping for breath.

"Save it, Jack...save it for Sarah. Love is what you *do*, not what you *say*, remember?"

I turned and stumbled out the garage door. I plopped my trembling body, along with my broken, devastated heart, into the car. Turning the ignition, the car started and the stereo came on. I quickly shut it off to hear myself think. As far as I was concerned, the music in my life was now gone.

I pulled out of that garage for the last time.

Jack stood there in total anguish, hands on his head and nearly naked. As I backed up, he closed his eyes and began to cry again. His frown made him look evil, and his nakedness made him look dirty. It was a completely different scene from just one day before.

As I drove home the only sound I initially heard was my own gasping for air. No more romantic ballads crooning from the stereo speakers, just a tear-soaked silence and a lonely road home.

And then the dam burst.

I cried. I wailed. I screamed. I wanted to run my car off the road and die.

How could I be so stupid? What have I done? What did I get myself into?

My tears fell like boulders onto my lap.

I looked down at my skirt. I had dressed in a hurry that awful morning and grabbed a skirt I hadn't worn in a very long time. Ironically, it was the very same tailored black-and-white skirt I had worn when Jack first kissed me. I had a closet full of clothes. What are the chances I would put on that skirt on this day, on a day that proved to be my defining moment? It was as if the skirt itself was telling the story.

When I arrived home I pulled into the garage and shut the door. Lowering the car windows, I sat there with my car running. I did not want to live. Not with this unbearable pain. The tears and makeup formed black paths down my face. I thought of all the lies I had believed. The promises I had embraced, now broken. Worst of all, I thought of how much I had trusted and loved him. I thought of how he stole my heart, only to throw it away.

Sin's seduction and its accompanying web of deceit were beginning to fade. The blindfolds I had placed on my eyes were ripped off and hanging around my neck. Ultimately, I had choked on deception and suffocated on duplicity. And now the noose had tightened as I was being strangled by my own treachery.

So it seemed only fitting that I should go out this way, choking and suffocating on toxic fumes. I prayed the exhaust from the car would quickly take my life so I wouldn't have to think anymore. Thinking was painful. Facing reality was agonizing. And the pain was excruciating. I didn't want to shut off the car, and I couldn't shut off my thoughts.

Oh God, let me die. I cannot live. My sin is too great. How will I face my children? How will I be able to go back to church? How will I face my friends? How could I have been so deceived?

*****

As I began drifting into unconsciousness, I saw in my mind a man in a white robe walking along the beach at sunrise. He bent down, and with his finger, he wrote in the sand. I did not know what the man wrote. But just then the tide washed up onto the sand and over the writing, and yet they could not erase what the man had written. Standing, he lifted his hands toward the heavens. A bold and bright sun burst forth up from the horizon, its vibrant colors illuminating his white gown. Then he spoke.

"Go now and leave your life of sin" (John 8:11).

I regained consciousness and knew that message was for me and that this was the dawning of a new day. Though the fumes were overwhelming, I somehow managed to turn off the car and stagger into the house. My body crashed, shutting down in an overwhelming sense of hopelessness. I was unable to work. I couldn't talk or get out of bed. I was defeated, spiritually bleeding and dying on the battle-field, crying out to God for help.[12]

In a moment I lost my best friend and the only man I ever loved. In that same moment I came face-to-face with my own hor-rific sin. I stood face-to-face with the reality that the man I trusted and allowed in my heart and life was living a double life. All along I surmised and knew about his infidelity issues. However, my own sin and involvement buried this reality, blinding me to it—that is, until that moment. Now I had a front row seat to what was real. Having now lost my present life, I was forced to face a painful past. The ques-tion was whether I could seek God enough to redefine my future.

*****

Jack Hardie had also met his match that day. This was one pickle he knew he could not talk his way out of. He knew I was not Sarah. Although I shared his guilt, he knew I would not put up with this

---

[12] Lysa Terkeurst talks about this deep emotion in her book *Becoming More Than a Good Bible Study Girl*: "But other times the hurt comes in the form of a loss that cuts into your heart so viciously it forever redefines who you are and how you think. It's what I call deep grief. The kind that strains against everything you've ever believed. So much so you wonder how the promises that seemed so real on those thin Bible pages yesterday could ever possibly stand up under the weight of your enormous sadness today." (Terkeurst, 144)

kind of reprehensible behavior. He would not be able to double-talk and obfuscate this one. He knew it was over.

So with nowhere else to go and devastated at his sinful exposure, Jack returned to Sarah at his Palm Beach home on that same day. Once again he was "discovered" with a woman and he returned home. He would try once again to convince Sarah into believing his version of the story.

Days and weeks passed. Jack continued to call to see how I was doing and to discuss our future. We cried and exchanged harsh and hurtful words as we both tried to write a new chapter in our lives. But my relationship with him was history. Finished. No matter how kind, generous, or persuasive Jack was, I would not allow myself to be deceived.

Not again.

Forgiveness

There's a well-known phrase that says, "Sin will take you farther than you ever wanted to go, keep you longer than you ever wanted to stay, and cost you more than you ever dreamed of paying." But it's more than just a phrase. It's a principle. Like gravity, it can be defied for a while but never fully escaped.

Succumbing to the powerful gravitational pull of sin's seduction always comes with a price. That reality caused me to be mad at myself for being so stupid. I was hurt for giving my heart, life, soul, and body to someone who could easily throw it away. I was ashamed of my actions and lifestyle. I was devastated at the person I had allowed myself to become. I could not understand how one person could have so much power over me to cause me to alter my entire life and belief system. I came to realize that this is the essence of spiritual seduction.[13]

---

[13] Beth Moore writes, "When Satan is trying to wreak havoc on the godly, he isn't always successful with a blatantly ungodly approach. Remember, we're talking seduction here. The nature of seduction implies an unexpected, well-disguised lure. Satan looks for ways he can get close to the godly and gain trust" (Moore, 40)

I was tormented by Jack's actions and with the pain reality can bring. Sexual sin is the only sin committed against your own body. All other sins are outside the body.[14] My heart was wounded, and I was emotionally bleeding out faster than I or anyone else could stop it.

This pain sent me into a downward spiral, resulting in depression. I went to the doctor and afterwards began seeing a Christian counselor. My life was reduced to work, home, and sleep. When I didn't have to go to work, I stayed in bed all day. I retreated from activities and was withdrawn from friends. I lost weight. Crying became the highlight of my day. If I was crying, it meant I was still alive and had feelings. And as long as I was alive and could feel, I felt I had a chance.

At work I kept all my emotions bottled up and stuffed deep inside me just to get through each day. The pent-up hurt, anger, pain, and transgression were all rolled into one, like a knot in my shoulders, only more real. During the day, I was on autopilot. However, the minute I left work and was alone in the car, the floodgates opened again. And it was uncontrollable.

I repeated the garage scenario for months. I wanted to die, and sitting in a car breathing exhaust fumes seemed the best method to me. Day after day I pulled into that garage, lowered the door behind me, and opened the car windows. I don't know how or why I managed to get out of the car each time. I don't know where the strength came from. But what I did know for sure was that no one knew the pain I was experiencing. And I couldn't shake the agony.[15] I was suffering alone. In silence. Every day and night.

*****

---

[14] 1 Corinthians 6:18

[15] Beth Moore says, "Stealing is a sin, yet if I stole one hundred dollars and then changed my mind, dumping the money in a garbage bin, in some respects I could walk away without taking the 'sin' with me. On the other hand, if I commit sexual sin, I have a much harder time dumping the garbage. Why? Because spiritually speaking, it got 'on' me somehow. The sin was against my own body and wields a much stronger staying power" (Moore, 24)

My children knew something was terribly wrong but didn't know the real reason behind my odd behavior. My daughter, Rachel, who lived in a different state, recognized a change in my voice on the phone day after day. For weeks I sought to hide the pain but was unsuccessful. Rachel's keen perception told her something wasn't right. She knew I owned a handgun and phoned Joshua, telling him to go to my house and take it away from me.

Through the church grapevine Joshua heard that Jack had returned home, but he had no clue as to what had transpired. Over the last two years Joshua never disclosed to Rachel anything he knew about my relationship with Jack.

Joshua came over and tried to talk to me during this time, but I remained speechless. He informed me that he heard Jack was home but that something was terribly wrong with him. The word was that he was withdrawn, quiet, and depressed. He wanted to know what had happened and tried his best to get me to open up, but all I could do was cry.

What can I tell him? I thought. *How can I talk about it? How can I tell my son I fell in love with a married man, who, by the way, was also my Bible study leader and mission partner? How can I admit such a horrific sin to him? How do I reveal that Jack Hardie was not who we all thought he was? How could I ever tell Joshua that I found a woman in Jack's bed? Who would believe such a bizarre story? I hardly believed it myself, and I was there!*

Unable to process any of this, I had no words for my son, only tears.

Though he still didn't know what had happened, he was sure of one thing—the mom he loved had become withdrawn and depressed and possibly even a potential risk to herself. So, for my own safety, he took the gun away from me. The very weapon that Jack had given me to use for my protection was now the very weapon I could use for my own demise.

Eventually, everyone became concerned about my emotional well-being and mental health. In response I backed away from family and friends so they wouldn't witness me plummet even further into depression. I didn't want to see or talk to anyone, so I retreated to my home sanctuary, never leaving my private hideaway except for work.

Then one day, in a moment of desperation, I again picked up the book *When Godly People Do Ungodly Things*. This time the book came alive for me. It was as if Beth Moore was in my home, talking to me, comforting me, and understanding everything I was going through. I felt like Beth Moore was now on the battlefield with me, picking up my wounded body. Her words served as a bandage to my broken heart. Her knowledge of Scripture became a healing balm to my mind. Her words of wisdom were medicine to my sick soul.[16]

This time the book made sense. It was filled with truth that opened my eyes wide. And with every page I turned, I encountered both the comforting and convicting reality of God's truth. It was as if Beth Moore was reading my mind, speaking about, and *to, my* life. I was reading about myself. As Beth herself would say, "I had been *had!*"[17]

*****

After a month of depression, sorrow, and pain, I was ready to talk and so I requested to meet with Colby; the four pastors of my church; Joshua and his wife, Shanna; and some of the church staff, including Dorothy. We all met together at Joshua's home one evening. Everyone wanted to know what was going on with Jack Hardie, the once missionary man and Bible teacher. They all knew I was the only one that had any answers. Kimberly, my best friend, had driven me there. With no other way home and a roomful of eyes staring at me, I realized I couldn't back out now.

Barely able to talk, I began confessing the whole story to them from beginning to end. I just wanted to come clean. No more lies. No

---

[16] Proverbs 16:24

[17] Beth Moore states that, "Many people who by the grace of God have never been 'had' by the devil wrongly assume that all departures from godliness are nothing but defiance, rebellion, and proofs of inauthenticity. They have no idea of the suffering involved when someone with a genuine heart for God slips from the path." (Moore, 13)

more hiding out. No more covering up. No more obfuscation. No more going back to Jack. I had come to realize that any relationship is wrong if you have to hide it. I wanted free from the relationship and the web of sin that had entangled my life. For me, there would be no more secrets because when it's not a secret, it has no power over me! This was my first big step toward what the Bible calls repentance.[18]

Though I couldn't fully explain it all to them, through my tears I was able to share the whole experience—all I had learned about Jack, myself, and what had come to light in the last month. I still did not understand Jack, his heart, or his motives; so I could not speak to that. But what I was able to do was tell them the truth. No more concealing! When I was finally able to look up at the group assembled there that evening, their faces were etched with astonishment. Some cried with me, they were all supportive of me and my restoration.

They too were shocked to hear of Jack's lies and cunning personality. After all they too had been tricked by him. It made them sorry for their own lack of discernment. Afterwards, they tried contacting Jack, to talk, but he would not hear of it. They went to his Palm Beach house but were unable to get beyond the gated driveway. The closest they got to talking to him was through the fence. But he made them leave, threatening to sue if they persisted.

---

[18] Beth Moore comments that, "Satan may work enough confusion to be able to delay feelings of repentance for a little while, but he cannot have his way for long. To anyone who has ever truly loved God, those feelings come all right. And when they finally come, the sorrow is almost unbearable." Ibid, 48.

30

Grace

One by one I began meeting with the people I had lied to and offended. I spoke with the leaders of the ministries with whom I had previously served. To my astonishment, they all graciously forgave me, expressing their love, and pledging their prayers for me as I moved forward.

I then spoke with Dorothy, our church's women's ministry leader I had avoided. She also forgave me, offering wise counsel instead of condemnation. This time I listened and even followed up with meeting a few more times for guidance and direction. I told her I was now reading the book she gave me, *When Godly People Do Ungodly Things*, and that I was receiving a newfound insight and hunger for direction.

I met with Donna and apologized for lying to her that day at Starbucks. I asked her to forgive me for talking badly about her. I admitted to her that she had been right about everything she said to me that day. I thanked her for being the only one who had the courage to confront me with love and kindness. I acknowledged how Donna's gentle words of correction had penetrated my soul, and that although I did not respond immediately to her words of wisdom, God had still used that meeting.

"Your confrontation that day repeatedly came to my mind during the most sinful moments in the weeks following our meeting," I revealed. At the time Donna's accusations made me angry and bitter. But they had also burdened my heart with extreme guilt, the healthy kind. Though I tried to disregard her spiritual correction, Donna had no idea the effect she had on me until now or how her words rang in my ears.

Donna responded by apologizing for bringing me to Starbucks under somewhat false pretenses. I assured her I understood she was resorting to extreme measures for the chance to confront me. It was an attempted intervention, and at the time I bolted in an effort to continue concealing my sin and preserve my lifestyle.

A precious few people know how to wisely and biblically confront this type of sin, especially within the church. Many are afraid of the repercussions of such a confrontation, the first one being, "What if the accusation is wrong?" Would the confrontation make the accused mad enough to leave the church and then slander the leadership?" Many times leaders (and even friends) are unwilling to take that risk. So they go on pretending, looking the other way, believing everything is fine, and possibly burying the truth even further.

The second possibility is, "What if the accusation is correct and the person does not stop the relationship?" Could the confrontation cause more harm now that their sin has been exposed? Unsure as to how to effectively confront another churchgoer or friend, they simply "pray from a distance."

However, the third possibility is, "What if the confrontation is correct and God uses the words of a friend to bring restoration?" That's what Donna did. It may not have brought instant sorrow, but God used Donna's words to reverberate in my mind. Her words were like a heavenly chisel that began chipping away at my hardened sinful heart.

Donna immediately accepted my apology, extending God's grace and mercy to me. She told me she was proud to be my friend and knew I was struggling with returning to church and facing the people who knew this story. She let me know she would be proud to sit next to me in church and be my friend. Donna had no idea what those words meant to me. I felt dirty…unworthy…worthless. I was so ashamed of what I had done and felt like everyone in church was looking at me with disgust (a ridiculous fear as very few people even knew what had transpired). Though still embarrassed about church, Donna's words of forgiveness and demonstration of kindness warmed my heart.

For me Donna is the true example of a what a Christian friend really is. She stepped out with courage and faith believing that God would use her, regardless of her own consequences. She confronted me with words of correction and then prayed I would live a godly life. She told me she had believed me when I claimed Jack and I were not intimately involved. Even so she continued to pray for me, unaware that God was slowly working on me. And when I finally confessed the truth to her, she chose forgiveness over judgment and again lifted me up in prayer. Donna would go on to walk with me throughout my entire healing process.

*****

I was encouraged by the love and grace shown to me by everyone with whom I had met. However, I had a feeling the next name on my list wouldn't prove to be as gracious. I was determined to meet with Sarah and plead for her forgiveness. However, I was unsure of quite how to do that. The sorrow and pain I felt for her was so great. I wanted to kneel at her feet, beg for her forgiveness, and explain how sorry I was, having caused her so much pain. I felt like a face-to-face meeting would be best; however, I didn't want to make things even worse.

I first tried sending her an e-mail, begging for her forgiveness. I thought perhaps that would be a nonthreatening start. So I sent the e-mail of apology, but Sarah never responded. Jack called me afterwards, informing me that he knew about the apology. I strongly suspected Jack had intercepted the e-mail as Sarah had always responded to me in the past.

*****

I then discovered through the church grapevine that Jack had immediately sold their Palm Beach home. It was on the market for almost two years during his planned divorce, but he had been unable to sell it. I was told that the house sold way below the asking price and that afterwards Jack and Sarah left town in a forty-five-foot coach motor home.

Jack had finally achieved his dream of running out of town in a motor home.

Following this, Jack called me again to see how I was doing and to get a pulse on my level of disclosure. He told me he bought the coach motor home from the same dealership we had visited together. He went back to John, the same salesman (as promised), and, of course, purchased the model with the two bathrooms, one in the back and one in the middle.

During that phone call, I asked Jack if he had confessed the truth to Sarah. He informed me that he would never tell Sarah the whole truth as he would always and forever protect *me*! I couldn't help but wonder if he was really protecting me or himself. After all Sarah had believed Jack to be impotent, so now she would also likely believe him when he returned home to say our "friendship" was over.

After traveling for the summer months, enough time for the church chatter to die down, Sarah and Jack returned to Palm Beach, moving into a beachfront condo. He called me again to see "how you're doing." An interesting question coming from a man who seamlessly transitioned right back to his former life. Jack was like Teflon. Nothing seemed to stick to him.

Hearing his voice, I thought, *How am I doing? He really just asked me that? He is living the dream he planned for us. He restored his life, going back to normal while I am left to pick up the pieces and face the pain, guilt, sin, and shame.*

He went back to his prior relationship…
I am left alone.
He is traveling in the motor home…
I am living in the same house.
He is living on the beach, in a condo, and watching the sunrise…
I am driving to the beach, sitting in a chair alone, and watching the sun come up.
He continues to obfuscate…
I have given up lying and concealing the truth completely!
He is still living a lie…
I am free from all the secrets and deceptions.

I could tell from our infrequent conversations that Jack had not changed. I never initiated contact with him again, though occasionally he called me. Answering the phone, I always hoped and prayed I would hear sorrow in his voice for our inappropriate relationship. But I never heard it.

"Hi, my Amber," he said, stumbling over his words. "I mean, Amber. It's Jack." His deep voice still sounded so caring, and it made my heart ache. "I just wanted to see how you were doing?"

My mind began swirling with all kinds of things to say. I missed talking to him, but I had nothing to say to him. I scrambled for something in response. "I'm okay," I lied. "How are you?"

"I am sad and depressed. I messed up bad. I have lost you forever," he said. His words hurt. I couldn't process his sincere-sounding words with what I knew was true about his character. He hesitated, then said, "I don't know if you heard yet, but we moved to a penthouse condo on Palm Beach Island."

My heart ached as I thought of him living out the dream he had promised me. However, I didn't want him to know how I was feeling. I curtly replied, "Yes, I heard."

He continued, "I sit on the west patio every night and watch the sunset over the city. I can't believe how much I appreciate sunsets now. They now have new meaning as I sit and watch the beauty unfold. Each sunset reminds me that there is hope for tomorrow." He hesitated and then his deep voice whispered, "Each sunset reminds me of you."

My heart sank as I held back the tears. I quickly changed the subject. "How are you and Sarah doing?"

"The same as always. Nothing has changed." His voice was grieved.

"Did you tell her about us?"

"Oh, my Amber, I, I mean, Amber." It was hard to know whether he was misspeaking on purpose or by accident. "I will never tell Sarah about us. She just thinks we were good friends, and that's it. She doesn't know about our intimate relationship. I will protect you till the day I die."

It made me sad to know that Jack was still living a lie and a double life. He never confessed anything to Sarah about our relationship or what drove him home on that May afternoon. I alone knew about the spiky-haired, half-naked blonde cuddling in his bed. As long as Sarah believed he was impotent, he feels he has nothing to confess. And as long as he has nothing to confess, he can continue hiding behind a false identity and his wife and continue with his sinful endeavors.

Though those who heard my confession had been forgiving, compassionate, and encouraging, I, on the other hand, was having a hard time forgiving myself. It had been made abundantly clear to me that I was my own worst enemy? I simply could not forgive myself. I felt like I needed to suffer. To pay for my crimes against God. Maybe if I cried enough that would do it. Or if my pain and guilt were severe enough. Sometimes I even wanted to die. I was still so angry at myself. I was trying to desperately rediscover my joy, but it had been taken from me. I wondered if I would ever find it again.

*****

About this time, my best friend, Kimberly, gave me some sound advice. "Look, Amber. Jack Hardie stole the last two years of your life from you. Don't let him steal the *rest* of your life too. Don't give him, and the past, permission to rob you of your happiness. He is living his life, fine. But now you have to live yours. *Don't let him win!*"

How I thank God for good friends like Kimberly. She made me leave the house…and cry. Kim made me go to the beach…and cry. She prodded me to go out to eat…and cry. And Kim cried with me as well. That's what good friends do. They listen…and cry with you.[19]

Though my healing had begun, many unanswered questions still lingered in my mind. I spent the next few months struggling with disbelief and confusion. I didn't know why I felt that way. Everyone told me that after what I had witnessed, I should be able to walk away easily. However, I couldn't shake all those unanswered questions: Were Jack's words really sincere promises or just lies all along? Was what we had real or fake? Was it love, or was it just a game to him? The pain of not knowing the answers to these questions continued fueling my tears.

I finally came to terms with the fact that I would *never* really know. There are moments when I think I have it all figured out. But just when I convince myself that Jack's love was all a lie—the pain caused by that lie makes me feel like it must have been true love. I figured that pretend love should only make me angry, while only real love can bring this kind of pain. The vicious cycle of confusion played in my mind day after day, swirling like a tornado and ripping my life apart.

For my part, it was real…but still wrong.

Regardless of Jack's heart condition during our relationship, *my* heart was motivated by emptiness and fueled by sin. I realized that only I was responsible for my own heart. I should have guarded and protected my heart as God's word urges me to do, but I didn't.[20] So I was left facing my consequences. Scripture warns us to flee from sexual immorality.[21] And there are good reasons for those commands. God's commands are always there to protect and provide for us.

---

[19] Romans 12:15
[20] Proverbs 4:23
[21] 1 Corinthians 6:18, 2 Timothy 2:22

When the heart, mind, and emotions are connected to physical feelings between two people, the bond goes deep. When the relationship turns immoral, guilt and shame are added to the pain of the loss. Whether an intimate relationship is within marriage or outside of it, when it ends it feels like a limb is being ripped off your body.

All during this healing period, people kept telling me it would get better. They said God would fill the empty spaces, that He has sifted me and now was refining me into a better person. However, I still felt like I was still in the sifting stage. Or more like I was being ground against a cheese grater, sliced into tiny pieces. I felt like Swiss cheese, and the tears flowed through the holes. The sword of His Word had wounded and penetrated my heart, and now I needed God to mend those wounds and fill the empty spaces in my heart... to heal the hurt.

My daily prayer was for God to heal the pain, fill the hole in my heart, restore my broken spirit, and mend my shattered life.

I had learned a harsh reality. As C. S. Lewis said, "A heart open to great love is also open to great pain." But an even deeper truth was that a heart open to sin is also vulnerable to great misery and devastating consequences.

*****

Months later I decided to take a giant step toward restoration by joining a ladies small group Bible study at church. I knew I wouldn't be "sharing" in the discussion, but I thought it might be a good way to reconnect with some church friends.

Although I was not talking about what happened between me and Jack, I knew Sarah, in the past, had been quite verbal to some people about her suspicions. For that reason I prayed that none of the ladies in this group would be privy to my "secret sin" and thus reject me. I wouldn't be able to take the judgment and ridicule. So my defenses were up as I approached the room that first night. Part of me wanted to turn around and go back home, but I managed to open the door and walk in without bursting into tears. That was a minor victory.

The first person I saw was Judy, Nick's wife. I knew Judy and Nick were about the only friends Jack and Sarah allowed to remain in their lives. I assumed Judy knew most of the story, and that made me want to turn and run. I was paranoid that Judy would announce to everyone the shame I was carrying. Judy looked up and spotted me with a look of surprise. I responded by hanging my head in shame.

Maybe I could sneak to the back of the room and sit far enough away and Judy would stay quiet. Maybe if I didn't make eye contact with her, then maybe she won't look at me with disgust.

But it was too late, while I was trying to figure out my next move, Judy stood to her feet. It was evident she was not going to remain quiet. Like a woman on a mission, she began walking toward me. My heart began pounding, and my body started to sweat. There was nowhere for me to run without making a scene.

Why did I think this was a good idea? What made me think a woman's Bible study would be a "safe" place to acclimate myself back into church? I was all too aware of how mean and judgmental women can be, so I braced myself for the attack I knew was coming. An attack I felt I deserved.

I felt my eyes swelling with tears. Judy and Nick were two of the nicest people I knew. At one time we were all friends, but I had let them down. I stood there, preparing for the worst.

Judy walked right up to me and looked right into my now tear-filled eyes. And then, unexpectedly, she wrapped her arms around me. We both stood there crying as Judy whispered in my ear, "I am so glad you are here, Amber. I am happy you came back to church. I love you." I could not believe what I was hearing. It was everything I *didn't* deserve—a warm welcome and unconditional love.

Her embrace was a beautiful picture of God's love. Judy was a true Christian woman and knew "the story." Yet she still loved me. It made me wonder if I could do the same for someone else who needed that kind of unconditional love.

That day God showed me His mercy through one of His precious servants. He took a horrific experience and used it to teach me grace, mercy, forgiveness, and love. As we stood there crying, I whispered back, "I am so sorry, Judy. I am so very sorry."

Judy pulled back and looked into my eyes. Her voice was confident as her face glowed with Jesus's love. "I know." She smiled at me. "I know...now come. Sit at my table. You can be in my group."

My heart was enlarged and overwhelmed with Judy's expression of love, forgiveness, and mercy. Each step toward that table was a step toward freedom. Judy could not have possibly known how much her act of kindness meant to me that evening. But it became another positive step toward healing. I sat down at her table with a broken heart and a new understanding of grace, not just of what it was but also what it felt like to receive it.

Restoration

The recurring mental picture of walking into Jack's bedroom on that awful morning still haunted me. I was angry at Jack for what he had done, but I was also mad at God for not sparing me the visual details of encountering that woman. I had fallen so far away from my relationship with God that I believed God was somehow to blame for my sinful pain. The mental picture of that woman in Jack's bed played over and over in my head. However, I soon realized that those visual details had actually revealed my own horrific sin.

I had so many questions pelting my mind like incessant raindrops. *Why? Why did this happen? Why did I meet Jack? Why did I fall in love with him? Why didn't anyone know the truth about Jack Hardie? And if they did, why didn't they tell me? How could I have been so blind to his real self? How could he manage to fool everyone and live such a double life? Why didn't anyone suspect or confront him? Why? Why? Why?*

It was at this time that I began reconnecting to Christian music. Music had always been such an integral part of my spiritual DNA and walk with God. But during my time with Jack, it had all but faded away, replaced by sentimental love songs and romantic ballads.

There was one particular song by MercyMe that I kept coming back to called "The Hurt and the Healer," reminding me of the truth that God has it all in his control.

"Find your glory even here." Those words marinated in my mind as the healing set in, softening my heart. I began to get an entirely new angle on my circumstances, seeing more of God's big picture. As time passed my initial anger at God subsided. Looking back, I now saw how He had tried to stop my actions and my ungodly relationship on many occasions. I thought back on Jack's cancer, the car accident, and the encounter with Sarah at the waterfront house in Fort Lauderdale. I remembered the visit from Donna and the meeting with the church pastors who attempted to intervene. But I didn't listen. I was blind and deaf to God's prompting in my life.

I came to realize what even baby Christians know, that you can't willfully reject fellowship with God and then expect Him to remain near. James 4:8 says, "Draw near to God and He will draw near to you." So it makes sense that if you are far from God, it is only by your own choice. As I confessed my sin and began seeking God on *His* terms, my intimacy with God returned and it showed in my actions.

As I allowed God to permeate my heart and every part of my life, my vision started to clear up and rational thinking was restored. Under normal conditions, if a married man tried to kiss me, I probably would have smacked him in the face and spit in disgust. That's why it made me wonder, *Why? Why did I allow it?* Also, had I not been so blinded by the ongoing, alluring effects of sin, I would have questioned his sincerity since I already knew about the extramarital affairs in Thailand. I should have recognized the red flag of his separate e-mail address. But I didn't. I was deceived by sin and by my own needy heart. And by definition, when someone is deceived, they don't realize it. Otherwise, they wouldn't be deceived! Jeremiah the prophet reminded me that the human heart is "more deceitful than all else, and is desperately sick; who can understand it?"[22]

I thought, as a single God-seeking woman, it would be easy to find the right man and weed out the wrong ones. They would

---

[22] Jeremiah 17:9

be obvious. I was not the type to go to a bar to find a husband as I had stereotyped such men to be promiscuous liars. I knew I would never go out with a man who did not have a strong relationship with God. I was seeking a man who would be my spiritual leader and counselor. That's the only kind of man who would have ever been on my radar.

I had no idea that men like Jack Hardie exist within the church. I was unaware that there are men who actually hide behind a relationship with God. They use God, ministry, mission trips, and even a good wife to cover their tracks. I didn't realize that men like Jack could be so cunning that they not only fooled the women they pursue, but also deceive their friends, church leaders, and pastors amid their indiscretions. I guess I was naïve that way.

Of course, I knew these types of men existed but only in scandalous tabloids, news headlines, or movies. But a man like that could never gain access to my life. He would never know my family, neighbors, friends, and even attend my church. He would never be a coworker or friend. No way he would ever be my church leader or Bible study teacher.

At least that's what I thought.

I never imagined this type of aggressive powerful man could never be so kind, generous, and sweet to me, my friends, and family. I assumed that this type of cunning liar would also be mean, abusive, and rough. It made no sense to me that a manipulative man would also be kind, sweet, caring, and generous. But again, isn't that inherent in the definition of *cunning* and *manipulative*?

The devil rarely uses the front door.

I learned that part of my healing process was learning to accept my own blame. I had no illusions about the fact that I was guilty of a grievous sin. No one forced or coerced me to do anything I did not want to do.

I now understood that on that dreaded May morning, God stepped out of heaven and said, "Enough! I will not let you live like this anymore." He knew I was so blind that I could no longer clearly see my own sin. I would have to experience the same pain, hurt, and sorrow I was causing Sarah in order to come to a place of true repentance, and not just verbal excuses.

God showed me that even though we don't deserve it, He will always leave the ninety-nine to find the one lost sheep. This is because His love knows no end. Instead of blaming God, I now saw that He loved me so much that He stepped out of heaven to intervene in my life! He truly was in control, even in my sin, causing me to show up at Jack's house that day, allowing me to have that horrific experience. In His providence, that moment proved to be a catalyst, putting me on the path toward freedom. I was now in awe of such sovereignty and loyal, steadfast love.

I don't see myself as a victim but rather a survivor. Yes, I could have easily chosen to wallow in my pain, sorrow, and despair, continuing to cry and be depressed. I could have turned to pills, drugs, or alcohol to relieve the pain. Or I could choose to live in His victory. Living in secret and burying the pain, or choosing freedom in Christ through experiencing His forgiveness.

By God's grace, I chose freedom…I chose forgiveness…I chose hope.

Like a shattered vase on a tile floor, I spent months picking up the pieces of my broken heart and damaged life. There were endless hours in counseling, trying to sort through the sin, pain, hurt, and sorrow. I longed to be the Amber I used to be. There have been many baby steps along the way toward my restoration, but my God has been with me with each step, walking close by my side.

My relationship with Jack was not the plan I had envisioned for my life, but I was learning to see that He can remake even the worst of our mistakes, "working all things together for the good" (Rom. 8:28 NASB). I had to yield to God's right to rule in my life. I was learning all over again what it meant to abide in Christ.

But this didn't mean my struggles instantly vanished. I still struggled with my fall from grace. It was a daily battle not to dwell on the past. I had to learn to slow down and meditate on God's goodness, not my past sin.

I posted a daily reminder for myself on the bathroom mirror:

"Joy—deep down confidence that God is in control!"

*****

The Grey Zone is not glamorous. It's not a place where we can find a worthwhile, meaningful relationship. On the contrary, it is a dangerous, volatile, and treacherous minefield of life that will eventually explode, killing parts of your life you will never be able to get back. You may come out alive but a part of you will definitely suffer and die. Of that you can be sure.

I have learned there are many shades of grey, and every one of them treacherous, no matter how harmless they appear. If you have to stop and think whether something is grey, then it probably is. And sometimes the lighter the shades of grey, the more dangerous they are. It's merely a gateway to a darker experience. The seemingly trivial temptations are those which often lead down the path to ruin. The Grey Zone may appear alluring, but it delivers destruction.

A very light shade of grey may be likened to a crack in a wall. The standing wall may still be able to keep out the wind, snow, and rain for a long period of time; but eventually that crack will leak, allow water in, and eventually it will freeze. The ice will cause the crack to spread. The crack will get bigger, and the cycle will repeat. After time the wall will have a hole in it. If left unrepaired, the wall will crumble and fall. The mightier the wall, the bigger the fall.

My experience taught me to no longer make my own plans and then ask God to bless those plans. My heart's desire was now to ask God for His plan and blessing, walking on the path He has ordained for me.

Through my failure, God got my undivided attention. He took me to a place of defeat in order to build something good in my life. I can now appreciate my "mountaintops" with God because of all my valleys spent without Him.

At any given time all of us are just one step away from sin, one choice away from stumbling and falling. In time, I was able to be grateful for my journey through the Grey Zone. I feel as though I've been to hell and back. As a result, I now have a keen awareness of God's voice and a sensitivity to His presence I never had before.[23]

In my counseling, I learned that "when it's not a secret, it has no power." Satan wants people to hold on to their secrets. He wants them live in shame and despair. Satan had robbed the last four years of my life. By God's power, I would refuse to give him my future.

---

[23] In, Becoming *More Than a Good Bible Study Girl*, Lysa Terkeurst defines contentment: "Maybe this is the true secret to being fulfilled and content. Living in the moment with God, defined by His truth, and with no unrealistic expectations for others or things to fill me up. Not reaching back for what was lost in my yesterdays. And not reaching for what I hope will be in my tomorrow. But living fully with what is right in front of me. And truly seeing the gift of this moment." (Terkeurst, 36)

Good-bye, Mr. Grey

Six months later, I asked Jack to meet me one last time. I knew this would be perceived as grey by some, but I needed closure and to write the final chapter in our story. I also wanted to tell Jack how I had confessed the whole truth about us to our pastors, family, and close friends. I felt empowered that the secret was out and that there were no more lies. During our phone conversations over the last few months, it was clear that Jack had no idea I had confessed the truth. I'm sure Jack thought I would take our secret to my grave.

But I also knew Jack well enough to realize he would not allow anyone to confront him about the past few years. No one would be allowed to hold him accountable for his double life. Some had tried, of course, but he refused to speak to any of them. Anticipating future confrontations was probably why he initially fled in the motor home and left town. I also knew he would continue lying to Sarah and that others would be hurt. Eventually, there would be another Amber, Chen, or Juanita in Jack's life. Being his last conquest, I wanted to stop this vicious, selfish cycle.

When Jack and Sarah left Palm Beach in their motor home, he cut all ties to our mutual friends and church leaders. He had no idea all of our church leaders and mutual friends now knew the truth. I was literally the only person he would agree to meet. Besides, I was pretty certain that if I started explaining true repentance to him over the phone, he would interrupt me and divert the conversation. After all he was still Jack Hardie and he still thought he was invincible. So this talk had to be in person, face-to-face.

Jack knew full well my fears about people discovering our relationship and how I had been careful to conceal our relationship during those two years. He knew I didn't like being out in public for fear of being seen together. He was also aware of how I had lied, denying our relationship to others. He knew that being seen as the "other woman" was repulsive to me. And he knew I wouldn't leave town with him until he was officially divorced. All this, I am sure, caused Jack to conclude that I would bury our murky secret relationship forever in the back of my mind. With this assurance, he would be able to keep obfuscating his way through life.

It would be difficult for him to accept the fact that I had come clean with the truth since he was still living a lie. Even after all that had happened, he was still lying to Sarah about us, convincing her we were no more than friends. After all Jack still occasionally called me.

It made me wonder if Jack could be changed, and if he would ever be able to grasp the concept of being free from himself. When caught in his sin, he cried and felt sorrow but I still wondered if he had ever experienced true repentance in his life. He was sorry he got caught, but he never expressed sorrow for our sinful relationship. On the contrary, he spun it into something good, even "godly." Jack had lived a lie for so long that it had become his normal, and I now knew what that felt like. But now I was free, and I wanted him to find the release from sin that can only come through true repentance before God.

He had pledged to always "protect" me by keeping the truth from Sarah, but I believe he was just protecting himself...and his sin. Jack wasn't in love with me; he was in love with himself. His motto had always been, "Love is what you *do*, not what you *say*." But it became clear to me that his real guiding principle was closer to, "I love *me*...and I want *you!*"

I no longer needed Jack Hardie's protection. God was now my Protector. But what I did need was a clear conscience. I needed to share with Jack what true love and forgiveness could do for him. I had been shown grace when I repented, and now I sought to extend that same grace and forgiveness to Jack.

Like I once was, Jack was on the battlefield alone. God had shown up for me that day when I discovered the blonde in his bed. I was hoping I could show Jack that God wanted to fight for him too, since no one else could get near him. I just wanted God to use me to speak truth into his life, just like Donna had done for me.

But in order to do this, I had to face him one more time.

I informed my counselor, Renee, of the plan to meet with Jack. I wanted her to be my accountability. There would be no more secrets and lies, so I wanted her to know about it. Renee advised against the meeting, warning me of the dangers of such an encounter.

"You know you are taking a chance by meeting up with him," she cautioned. "Your heart is still beating... and bleeding with mixed feelings of confusion. You are still healing from your wounds. I know you have come a long way in your understanding of this relationship. However, you also know the power this man has had over you in the past."

I stared out the window, at the rain, while my mind seesawed back and forth. "I know, Renee. I know you are right. At this point, seeing him again may stir up feelings of caring and tenderness, or perhaps hatred and hurt." I concentrated on the slow, steady rhythm of the rain. "But I won't really know until we talk." Then, looking intently at her, I confidently asserted, "However, what I know with all my heart is that Jack is lost. He is struggling and on a battlefield all alone with his sin. No one knows him, and his battle, like I do. He continues to cover up and live a lie. There is no one that can even get close enough to speak truth into his heart and life."

A distant bolt of lightning lit up the sky followed by the rumble of thunder that rattled her office windows.

"When Donna spoke the truth to me that day at Starbucks, I didn't respond well. But the truth still penetrated my heart and pricked my conscience. When Judy extended grace to me, it helped to set me free from my bondage to sin. All I know for sure is that I have to lead by example and hopefully extend the same grace and truth to Jack. Maybe, just maybe, if I do that, he can be saved from himself and a lifetime of lies."

"I know your heart, Amber, and I know you mean well," Renee said authoritatively. "But I just worry about you. I worry your heart will get pulled back in."

"Oh, Renee, believe me, after what I have been through..." My eyes locked on hers. "Don't worry, I *will* walk away!"

Renee managed an encouraging smile, nodding her head in agreement. I was grateful for her concern as I knew she genuinely cared about me. She had been a solid counselor and one who cheered me on throughout my healing process.

The rain was still coming down hard as I left her office that afternoon, but I was optimistic that the storm would pass, and Florida's bright blue skies would soon return.

*****

The next day I phoned Jack, and he agreed to meet me in public, in a local parking lot. We pulled up next to each other and rolled down the windows. Immediately, my body began to quiver, causing me to hesitate. So confident the day before, I now wondered if I was doing the right thing. We just sat and looked at each other through the open car windows. I had not seen Jack since that dreaded early morning trauma. An unexpected panic crept up on me as I felt my heart begin to melt into his eyes. I had forgotten what I used to feel every time I looked at him, and I was not prepared for him to still have that kind of power over me.

"Amber, why don't you come get in the car with me?" he suggested.

I had planned for him to get into my car, thinking I would be more in charge of the meeting. I wondered if Jack suspected I might have ulterior motives, or even that I might try and do him harm. He didn't know Joshua had taken my gun from me.

I conceded and methodically slipped out of my car and walked around the back of his to get in the passenger's side. Jack leaned over to open the door.

Sitting in the front seat of his car, my mind was flooded with memories. So much had been discussed in that car through the trips and outings we'd taken. *Just hold it together*, I told myself.

"Hello, Amber, it's so good to see you again," Jack said in his familiar solemn, deep voice. He looked as handsome as ever, though he had lost some weight and cut back his thick silver/black hair. I had never noticed before, but his hair was clearly turning more and more silver. He was nicely dressed, as if he were going out on a date, and the recognizable aroma of his cologne brought back a thousand memories.

My heart broke at the loss of what once was a dear friend. I tried holding back the tears, but they were already welling up in my eyes. Looking into his blue eyes, I managed a whisper. "Thank you for meeting me," I said, swallowing hard. I could feel my lips quivering.

Jack reached over, twirling my black curly hair gently in his fingers. He pushed it away from my face and behind my shoulders to see me better. I looked down to gain my composure as my eyes began to burn. He tenderly touched my face and caressed my shoulder. He was being "Jack" again. Nothing had changed on his end. Was he trying to romance me back to him? What was his angle here? What was his motivation? Turning to face him, I wanted to speak, but he beat me to it.

"I can't believe you are really here in front of me. You look great, Amber. Your hair got so long, and you look so thin. How much weight did you lose?"

I didn't answer. I wasn't about to tell him how devastating the last six months had been to me and what a toll it had taken on my health. His gentle touch brought back so many memories, and his deep voice melted my heart. I could sense old familiar emotions rising within. I took a deep breath, remaining strong…and emotionally detached.

Looking up at him, I stared into his bright blue eyes. My voice was soft but now more steady. "Jack, first you need to know how sorry I am to have entered into a relationship with you. I want you to know that I forgive you, and I am also asking you for your forgiveness. Please forgive me."

Through my counseling I had come to realize that I could not blame Jack for everything. It takes two people to have a relationship, and I was guilty too. He never forced me to do anything. I could have said no, but instead, I "followed my heart" and made all the wrong choices.

Jack looked perplexed, and it was confirmation to me that godly sorrow and true repentance was a foreign experience to him. His face remained solemn. His blue eyes were sad but fixed on my every word.

"Yes, of course, Amber. I forgive you," he replied.

I sensed he was wondering why I would feel bad about "being in love." However, he seemed anxious to hear what I would say next.

"Jack, there is something you need to hear from me, before you hear it from anyone else." I unfolded two pieces of notebook paper on which I had carefully written everything I wanted to say. "I didn't want to forget anything, so please humor me and just listen as I read."

Jack appeared puzzled but listened. I knew I would be quite nervous and would not be able to say everything I wanted him to hear. I also knew this would be the last time we would see each other, so I had to be sure no stone was left unturned. By this time, I was shaking and crying as I began reading to him my story of confession and redemption.

As I read I begged him to also repent. Jack listened politely and did not interrupt me at all. I explained how there is freedom when we repent and no longer keep secrets but that mere worldly sorrow will only end up killing him. True love means obeying God, because God is love. His commands don't hinder us. They only give us freedom.

I begged Jack to come clean and be honest with Sarah and to no longer hide behind his lies. I knew Sarah would forgive him and stand beside him once she knew the truth about his struggles. I rehearsed how she forgave him after the car incident and even after she found the two of us together at the Fort Lauderdale house. Sarah also forgave him when he came crawling back home, even though they had started the divorce proceedings.

Continuing to read, I also told him that until he was able to face his issues, he would never truly be free. He would always be tormented by his past. That without confession and help, he would always be susceptible to the demonic forces that lead him to his temptations.

My heart was broken for my former friend. I admitted I was angry with him for the way he had violated our relationship with that woman. But now I was no longer angry with him. I just wanted him to openly apologize and find freedom in God. I silently prayed as I read, hoping I could be a similar voice of truth as Donna had been to me. After all God loved Jack as much as he loves me.

Jack didn't say a word, but instead allowed me to read each sentence without interrupting or questioning what I was saying. He sat there. I did not look up or hesitate as I read but just kept reading and flipping pages filled with emotion and truth.

I revealed to him how I had met with our pastors, the church leaders, Colby, Donna, Joshua and Shanna, confessing our sordid, sinful relationship. I told him I admitted to originally lying to Colby, the pastors, and to Donna when they confronted me. I explained that because of this, he didn't have to cover for me anymore as I was now free from the lies. Finally, I let him know how good it felt to be honest and not live a double life. I admitted to him that I was now in counseling and on a path of healing, restoration, and recovery.

When I finished reading, I looked up into his bright blue eyes. They were saturated with pain and sorrow. That was understandable, though I hoped he was sorry for all the right reasons.

Jack was quiet and somber for a few seconds, gazing down into his lap. Then he looked up at me as if a light bulb had illumined in his head. He slowly sat up straight in his seat. I could tell he was processing the information, and yet I braced myself, not knowing what he was about to do or say. He was visibly distressed, and his deep, steady voice cracked.

"Did you tell them about how you found me...and *her?*"

My heart sank and my stomach turned as the tears ran down my cheeks. That gut-wrenching experience of seeing another woman in his bed was forever etched in my mind. It represented a critical crossroads in my life, as I came face-to-face with the reality of my own horrific sin. In earthly terms, you could say it was the worst day of my life. But from a spiritual perspective, it was the day God stepped out of heaven and intervened, liberating me from the sin that had been held in bondage. I took a deep breath, returning the steady stare into his eyes. In slow motion, I sluggishly nodded in the affirmative, whispering, "Yes."

His face was stern, and I realized he had aged drastically since I had seen him six months ago on that sickening day. The color drained from his face, and he slowly looked away, closing his eyes, and sighing. We sat in silence as he processed my story of repentance and revelation of sin. It was clear to me that he did not know what to do with truth, and I didn't know what to do next.

Jack began shaking his head from side to side in slow motion. He let out a deep breath, then expelled air puffing his lips outward. "Well, I have to give you credit for coming to me in person to give me this news."

He was not happy, and it was apparent that he was not used to being confronted with his sin. Looking back at me, his blue eyes locked on mine. This time his voice was steady and firm.

He simply said, "Good-bye, Amber. Good-bye."

Epilogue

The trauma of Jack's good-bye that day shot pain throughout every bone in my body. My heart was broken, my mind in turmoil. Tears uncontrollably burst from my eyes, but not tears of sorrow. No, it was more like a cleansing, a deliverance. I could feel the life of my previous lies melting away. The last of my chains were falling off. I was finally, and completely, free. No more lies. No more obfuscating. No more hiding.

The battle for my heart, soul, and life was won! I was officially out of the Grey Zone. I placed a quivering hand on the car door, opening it. Turning, I looked one last time into Jack's bright blue eyes, the tears still streaming down my face.

"Good-bye, Jack. Good-bye."

I was a wreck, but I was free. I feared I would faint in the parking lot as I walked toward my car and off this spiritual battlefield—broken, bruised, and recovering from wounds...but alive. Starting my car, I realized the stereo was still tuned to Jack's favorite music station. I reach up and switched the preset back to my Christian radio station, and to my surprise, my favorite new song was playing. As I listened to Plumb sing, "I Need You Now (How Many Times)," I sang those words to God, meditating on how everyone has their own story filled with both hurt and beauty. I cried out the words to that song. "Oh God, I need you. I need you now. I am free!" I got my music and my life back the same day.

I drove out of that parking lot and glanced in the rearview mirror. He was still there, sitting in his car. But Jack was now in God's hands. I simply prayed that the words I had spoken would somehow convict Jack and bring him to repentance. But that was his decision, not mine. He was now, and would forever be, in my rearview mirror, along with the Grey Zone.

*****

Immediately following that day, Jack and Sarah left town for good. They sold their penthouse beach condo in Palm Beach, the waterfront house in Fort Lauderdale and, the real estate businesses along the east coast, disappearing from the radar and dropping all contact with our mutual friends.

I revisited Jack's favorite motto and decided to make my own definition of love. Instead of "Love is what you do, not what you say," my guiding principle became, "Love is…a *commitment* to do what is best for the other person, actively and sacrificially, regardless of feelings without expectations of getting anything in return!"

*****

Now that Jack had moved off the beach, I felt free to now move to my own condo there. There I could think of how I might tell others of the warning signs of the seduction of sin and the devastating consequences of romancing the Grey Zone. If it's true what they say, that nothing is wasted with God, then surely my story could warn and inspire others. I was now out of the grey and walking in the light and it felt so good to be home, both figuratively and literately.

The beach, my happy place. As I walked down to the edge of the water, I pondered the meaning of my name. Amber, a precious jewel. I was confident that my name was given to me for a reason. God loves me. (*Psalm 139:13 says, "For you created my inmost being; you knit me together in my mother's womb."*) Gratia just happens to be my perfect surname. It is the Latin derivative of "Grace." I am saved by God's grace. (*Jeremiah 29:11 says, "For I know the plans I have for you,' declares the Lord, 'plans to prosper you and not harm you, plans to give you hope and a future.'"*) My name is a reminder that nothing is a surprise to God. I was created from birth with a plan and a purpose. My walk through the Grey Zone did not change that. My journey still has a plan and a purpose.

Sitting on the beach, with newfound freedom and confidence, my earplugs playing Lauren Daigle's "You Say" ("In You I find my worth, in You I find my identity"), the gentle Florida breeze on my face and the sand under my feet, I reached for my pen, said a prayer, and slowly began to write:

"The Grey Zone is that spot between absolute right and absolute wrong..."

Bibliography

Blackaby, Henry T., and Richard Blackaby. *Experiencing God Day by Day*. Nashville: B&H, 1997.

Calhoun, Adele Ahlberg. *Invitations from God*. Downers Grove, IL: Intervarsity Press, 2011.

Moore, Beth. *When Godly People Do Ungodly Things*. Nashville: B&H Publishing Group, 2002.

Terkeurst, Lysa. *Becoming More Than A Good Bible Study Girl*. Grand Rapids: Zondervan, 2009

About the Author

Carolyn Joy lives in sunny Naples, Florida, where she enjoys kayaking, jogging, long walks, and sunsets. In her quiet time she enjoys reading, writing, and journaling. She has published two devotional journals, *The Overflow of the Heart* and *Let Your Heart Overflow with Joy*, which are available on all online bookstores. She has three married children, and she has been blessed with eleven grandchildren in eight years.

CPSIA information can be obtained
at www.ICGtesting.com
Printed in the USA
LVHW010011100221
678884LV00004B/403